"Derek's here to learn all the different aspects of the clinic's mission and duties. I think starting here would be beneficial for him," Gwen told Mya, the cook, before turning her gaze to Derek, prepared to see anger or disbelief in his expression.

Instead, amusement danced in his green eyes. Gwen blinked as confusion scattered her train of thought. Giving herself a mental shake, she said, "Each team member takes a turn helping in the kitchen. We feed not only ourselves but the whole village when we are here."

"Sounds like a plan," he said. "So, Mya, how can I help?"

Gwen watched the intense way Derek listened and asked questions as Mya explained the process of feeding an entire village of people. Pleasure swelled in her chest. He really was interested in what they were doing. That was good. Really good.

Showing him the importance of the work would be that much easier.

And keeping a professional attitude toward him that much harder.

Books by Terri Reed

Love Inspired

Loves Comes Home #258
A Sheltering Love #302
A Sheltering Heart #362

Love Inspired Suspense

Strictly Confidential #21

TERRI REED

grew up in a small town nestled in the foot-hills of the Sierra Nevada. To entertain her-self, she created stories in her head and when she put those stories to paper, her teachers in grade school, high school and college en-couraged her imagination. Living in Italy as an exchange student whetted her appetite for travel, and modeling in New York, Chicago and San Francisco gave her a love for the big city, as well. From a young age she attended church but it wasn't until her thirties that she really understood the meaning of a faith-filled life. Now living in Portland, Oregon, with her col-lege-sweetheart husband, two wonderful chil-dren, a rambunctious Australian shepherd and an array of other critters, she feels blessed to be able to share her stories and her faith with the world. She loves to hear from readers at P.O. Box 19555 Portland, OR 97280.

A Sheltering Heart

Terri Reed

Steeple
Hill®

Published by Steeple Hill Books™

STEEPLE HILL BOOKS

Steeple
Hill®

ISBN-13: 978-0-373-81276-9
ISBN-10:   0-373-81276-0

A SHELTERING HEART

Copyright © 2006 by Terri Reed

www.SteepleHill.com

Printed in U.S.A.

He who believes in Me, as the Scripture said,
"From his innermost being shall flow
rivers of living water."

—*John* 7:38

For my children.
Thank you for teaching me how to be a mother
and for blessing me with unconditional love.
Leah and Lissa, as always, you rock!

Chapter One

Gwen Yates checked the brown leather-banded watch on her wrist. Again. "Where are they?"

Okay, so it had only been all of thirty seconds since the last time she checked but still…where were her boss and his son? The group's flight would leave in less than twenty minutes and they all still had to get through security.

Her gaze scanned the crowded, sun-drenched Seattle airport terminal, searching through the throng of travelers for Dr. Ross Harper's distinctive white hair and towering frame.

"Probably stuck in traffic," offered Gwen's colleague, Joyce Kincaid.

The tall, athletic woman stood guard over her duffel bag and leaned against the wall of windows separating the foot traffic and the gift shop of SeaTac Airport. Joyce's short brown hair stuck out in tufts from beneath the brim of a khaki-green hat. She held a medical journal on childhood diseases.

Gwen admired Joyce's dedication in keeping abreast of changes in her field of pediatrics. Though Joyce had ten years on Gwen, they shared a bond of determination to be the best they could be in each of their chosen fields.

Ned Leeds, another colleague, nodded his balding head. "Monday morning. Slow commute."

His distinct abrupt way of communicating never failed to astound Gwen, even though his estimate was more than accurate for the Seattle traffic. The short, forty-something surgeon had made it clear in the beginning of her tenure at Harper

Clinic that he didn't waste his breath on trivial conversation. In the three years since Gwen had joined their clinic's staff as a physician's assistant, she had yet to hear the man say more than a four-word sentence.

Gwen turned her gaze back toward the ticket area. Dr. Harper would have allowed time for traffic. Something wasn't right. She toyed with the boarding pass in her hand. "Hey, Craig, do you have your cell on you?"

The fourth member of their team sat on the floor with his back against the wall. Craig Samuels, a twenty-five-year-old intern at Harper Clinic, reached into the outside pouch of the backpack sitting beside him and pulled out a small black flip phone. "Hit number three to auto-dial the doc's cell."

As Gwen flipped the phone open, the gate agent announced their flight to London would board soon. Her stomach contracted with anxiety. Where was Dr. Harper? Usually, her boss was prompt and expected others to follow suit.

She listened to the phone ringing. He was probably late because of his son, Derek, the unexpected add-on to this trip.

Gwen didn't agree with her boss that the new CEO of Dr. Harper's brainchild, Hands of Healing International, should join the team on this particular mission. Son of the founder notwithstanding, the man hadn't even been in his position for more than six months and had failed to show up on time to the training classes to boot.

Gwen had received the disturbing impression that Derek was only biding his time, trying to please his father, until something bigger and better came along.

Gwen's limited dealings with Derek, Dr. Harper's only child, had left an indelible impression. There was a recklessness to him that was disturbing, and she didn't like his intense way of looking at her as if she were some unexplainable virus strain that needed to be studied.

Not to mention the undercurrent of competition that charged the air whenever he was present. She had no clue what prize he wanted, but she'd decided not long after he'd come aboard that minimal contact was the best option.

"Harper."

The deep male voice rattled Gwen from her thoughts.

Derek.

"Where are you?" she asked.

"Just pulling up. There was an accident on I-5."

Thankful Dr. Harper and his son weren't the ones in the accident, she let out a relieved breath. "We're waiting at the security checkpoint."

"See you in a few." The phone went dead.

Gwen snapped the small handheld phone closed and handed it back to Craig. "They're on their way."

Joyce pushed off from the wall and snagged her duffel bag by the strap. "Let's get in line."

The rest of the group picked up their bags and moved to the end of the long line of people waiting to enter the roped-off area for the security check.

Craig tried to reassure Gwen. "No need to worry. They'll make it."

Gwen nodded and followed the others to the line, her own backpack gripped in one hand. Their carry-on luggage held their personal items while the baggage they'd all checked would transport the medical supplies they'd need in Africa.

Her anxiety eased a bit as she stood at the end of the security line. She knew what to expect on her third trip as part of Hands of Healing International.

On the long flight to London she planned to rest, listen to a variety of music on her iPod and sleep with the help of an eye mask and a squishy pillow she'd tucked into her backpack.

After a twenty-hour layover in London they'd board another plane, then land in Kampala, Uganda, and from there they'd take a transport to the small province of Moswani, located at the southwestern corner of Uganda, bordering Rwanda.

This trip would be unusual in several ways, most importantly because Derek

Harper was coming to shadow his father and learn firsthand the administrative needs of the ministry his father had started sixteen years earlier.

She looked forward to proving to Dr. Harper that she was ready to lead her own team on a Hands of Healing mission as they'd discussed several times over the last few months. Dr. Harper had indicated that this trip would be Gwen's time to be in charge of the medical personnel while Dr. Harper showed his son the meaningfulness of the work.

Gwen was grateful her dealings with Derek would be minimal. He made her uncomfortable, not in a sleazy way, but in a strange, unfamiliar way that left her feeling vulnerable and self-conscious. She didn't like the feelings at all.

"Harper."

Ned's low warning in Gwen's right ear invaded her space and made her quickly step back. For a breathless moment she rocked off balance onto the heels of her tennis shoes.

But then a big, strong hand grasped her

elbow, pushed her slightly forward, back on to firm footing, holding her until her world steadied. She quickly extracted her elbow from the strong grip.

"Thank you," she murmured as she turned her gaze to her rescuer and met vivid green eyes.

Tall, blond and amused, Derek Harper cocked a tawny brow at her. "Too much coffee?"

Her tongue stuck to the roof of her mouth for half a second before she regained her composure. "I don't drink coffee."

"Ah. Maybe you should." He turned his attention to the others. "Good morning all. I guess we're really going to do this."

Joyce smiled. "So glad to have you along, Derek."

Gwen stared at the slightly interested gleam in Joyce's blue gaze. Surely Joyce wasn't falling victim to Derek's surfer, beach-bum good looks.

Gwen gave a mental shrug. She certainly didn't care if Joyce set her sights on Derek. Romantic relationships were the last thing on Gwen's mind. They were too unpredictable and too easy to lose control of.

As Derek shook hands with Craig and then Ned, Gwen asked, "Where's your father?"

"He and Mother are coming."

Gwen raised her brows. "Your mother's coming on the trip?" That was also new and unusual.

From what Gwen had gathered over the years, Sally Harper didn't travel—something about a fear of flying—even though she supported her husband's vision of spreading God's word through providing medical services to those in need.

Derek's gaze bored into her. The quick negative shake of his head left her bewildered. In the past, Mrs. Harper said her goodbyes at home.

Gwen rationalized that since both son and father were traveling on this trip that Mrs. Harper had decided to see them off. Not so unusual in the grand scheme of things, she supposed. Gwen really liked her boss's unassuming and soft-spoken wife.

A small gasp from Joyce alerted Gwen's sense of unease. The little hairs on the back of her neck prickled.

"Here they are," Derek said and moved aside so they could be joined by Dr. and Mrs. Harper.

Gwen echoed Joyce's gasp and shock skipped up her spine to settle in a pounding beat behind her eyes. She blinked. But what she saw in front of her didn't change.

Dr. Harper sat in a wheelchair. The left pant leg of his dark cotton slacks had been cut away from the knee to the toes, exposing a hard white cast. His wife, looking tired, pushed the wheelchair. She was dressed in a comfortable knit two-piece suit in a demure green that brought out the color in her green eyes. Her blond hair was pulled back in a cropped ponytail.

"What...what happened?" Gwen ducked under the rope and moved to Dr. Harper's side.

Dr. Harper gave a rueful laugh. "Tripped over the dog in the middle of the night and fell down the stairs."

"Nearly gave us a heart attack," Sally piped up, placing her hand on his shoulder in a gesture of affection.

"Did you break a bone? Is it serious?"

"A hairline fraction of the tibia. I'm fine. It'll heal in no time."

"So you're okay to travel, right?" Gwen asked, her gaze searching Ross Harper's lined face.

He shook his head. Regret shone bright in his eyes. "No. Which is why I needed to talk with you all before you leave."

Gwen's gut clenched. The situation was spinning out of control. She detested not being prepared for change. She liked life to be predictable and orderly. Though medicine was a practice, procedures and step-by-step instructions kept the unexpected in check. "We should postpone the trip."

Dr. Harper took Gwen's hand, the warmth and assurance in his touch calming. "You all still need to go. Family in Crisis is expecting you."

Their partner organization in Africa had spent money, time and effort in bringing medical personnel to the undeveloped region of Moswani. Hands of Healing had made a commitment. Gwen understood that they had to keep that commitment. She returned to her place in line.

Her mind whirled with the implications of Dr. Harper not joining them. Would she be in charge? Would she be expected to take on the role of administrator, as well? Did Dr. Harper have that much faith in her?

She sent up a silent prayer of thanks to God for the opportunity He'd presented her. She'd make sure not to disappoint Dr. Harper's trust.

Dr. Harper quickly talked to the group, telling them they would be fine without him because they'd all been on similar missions before and he had no doubts that they'd do splendidly. They could expect a great deal of help from Family in Crisis. He appointed Gwen lead medical personnel.

Even though Gwen knew it was more out of necessity than confidence in her ability—she didn't have a specialty the way Joyce or Ned did and Craig was too inexperienced—she was pleased.

"So, Derek, this should be an adventure for you," Craig stated with a wide grin.

Gwen's gaze jumped to Derek's. For a fraction of a second she could have sworn she saw hesitation in his eyes before he nodded.

"Yes, and any help you can give me will be appreciated."

"You stick close, I'll show you the ropes," Joyce practically purred.

Gwen frowned. What role would Mister CEO play if his father wasn't coming to keep him occupied?

They moved collectively forward, inching closer to the no-return zone. Gwen's palms began to sweat. This wasn't how it was supposed to go. Dr. Harper should be leading the way.

"Can we say a prayer?" she asked, needing strength and clarity.

Dr. Harper gave her a pleased smile. Across the security ropes the team members joined hands. Gwen held her hand out to Derek. With a slight frown and quick glance around, he slipped his hand around hers. Dr. Harper intoned a prayer for a safe and successful journey.

"Uh, hmm." The security attendance cleared his throat, signaling they were next to pass through. Dropping hands, they each showed their IDs and tickets.

"Here we go. See you, Doc," Ned said as he stepped up to the security post, deposited his bag on the conveyor belt for screening. He stepped through the metal detector and went to collect his bag. Craig and Joyce followed Ned. They cleared security and headed for the gate.

"Bye, Doc," Joyce said with a wave. "See you in two weeks."

Gwen stood by, allowing others to go through, as Derek hugged his parents. Derek hefted his big black satchel over his shoulder and slipped under the rope. "Coming, Gwen?"

Dr. Harper waved off his son. "You go ahead. I need a word with her first."

"Okay." To Gwen, he said, "See you on the other side."

"Gwen, I need a huge favor," Dr. Harper said as soon as his son was through the metal detector and fading into the crowd.

"Anything."

There were very few people in her life she respected or trusted as much as her boss. Under his tutelage she was learning about medicine as well as life. He was a man who lived his faith.

"I need…*we* need…" He paused and took his wife's hand. "We need you to show Derek what the true purpose of Hands of Healing is—that we heal more than just bodies on these trips. Through Jesus's love, we heal hearts, as well."

Wishing she could sit down, Gwen shifted her feet as the weight of Dr. Harper's request pressed on her shoulders. "Wow. That's a big order, Doc."

"I know and I'm sorry for that." His lined face showed his concern. "This isn't the way I envisioned Derek's first trip."

"Sometimes God's plan is better," Sally stated softly.

A sinking feeling descended in Gwen's stomach. Looked as if she was going to be spending a lot more time with Derek than she'd first thought. "I can only promise that I'll try."

Dr. Harper squeezed her hand. "That's all we can ask."

With a wan smile, she said goodbye and went to join her team.

Derek Harper stood and stretched his legs, thankful he'd paid to upgrade his coach ticket to first class. He couldn't imagine cramming his six-foot-two-inch frame in a coach seat for an eight-hour transatlantic flight.

Walking down the aisle into the coach section, he noted that the others didn't seem to mind the less comfortable accommodations of coach. Whatever.

Craig was reclined against the bulkhead with headphones on and his lips moving to the music of his portable CD player. Joyce was farther back on an aisle seat with her nose buried in the book he'd seen her reading earlier. And Ned sat in the far back and looked to be flirting with the flight attendant who was busy getting the refreshments ready.

He thought it curious they didn't sit by each other. But then again, knowing they'd all be living closely together for the next two weeks, a little space on the flight probably was a good idea.

Not that he would be staying at the camp for the full two weeks. He had a marathon to win.

He was disappointed his father wouldn't be there to greet him at the finish line as they'd talked about. Part of his father's argument for Derek coming on this mission trip was that Derek could enter the elite African marathon scheduled for next week and his dad would be there to see it. Having his father watching and cheering him on always boosted his drive to win.

Without his father's presence in the

camp, though, he'd be able to slip away to train more often than he'd anticipated, which could increase his odds of winning.

Providing the redhead his father had put in charge didn't have a problem with Derek taking off, that is. Though he doubted she would. He was only going to be in the way, considering he had no idea what to expect or how he'd be able to help. He was a businessman, not a doctor, after all. This was supposed to be an opportunity to stand back and observe—learn what he'd be administrating.

But playing along and doing what he could would go a long way to cementing the bond with his father.

Derek stopped at the aisle where Gwen reclined against the window, her head resting on a bright yellow pillow and her long red braid dangling over her shoulder. Her pale, freckled face was relaxed and her dark lashes rested alluringly against her cheek.

He wasn't sure what to make of the woman. The few times he'd encountered her at the clinic she'd been all business.

Suddenly she opened her eyes and focused her unblinking amber gaze on him. He had the feeling she didn't let down her guard even in sleep. He smiled. She didn't.

Time to retreat, because he didn't want to upset the balance of things just yet. He had a strong suspicion that his plans for finagling extra training time were going to take all his charm to keep the boss lady from interfering.

Gwen disembarked from the plane at Heathrow Airport in England with the other weary passengers. As accommodating as the airline was, she welcomed the relief of standing and walking. Her mouth felt as if she'd swallowed cotton. Long flights always depleted the moisture from her body. The flight, thankfully, had been uneventful and surprisingly restful. She'd managed to sleep for part of the way.

The only unsettling event had been when she'd found Derek standing in the aisle watching her sleep. He'd just smiled before returning to his own seat in first class. She didn't know what to think about him or his strange behavior.

She'd been a bit miffed at first when he'd stated he didn't "do" coach. But after thinking the situation through she realized the coach seating would be uncomfortable for someone so tall.

Plus she knew from various overheard snatches of conversations of the staff— hard to not overhear in such a small, contained atmosphere—that Derek was a successful world-class runner.

She shuffled out of the Jetway and spotted her team waiting by a large pillar.

Her team. She liked the sound of that.

She didn't feel she'd proven herself to Dr. Harper well enough yet, but he must have some confidence that she could handle the mission, which really felt good.

As she approached the group she heard Joyce say, "I'm so glad we have this layover. Usually, we have to rush from one flight to another."

"Hey, Gwen, where are we staying tonight?" asked Craig. He looked rumpled and in need of a shave.

"We're booked at The Lodge hostel near Paddington Station. It's a short Tube ride."

"Oh, goody. The tube," Ned said dryly.

Gwen knew the surgeon wasn't fond of the London subway any more than he was of the New York one. He'd grown up in a borough of New York City but had moved to the Pacific Northwest to get away from the urban life.

Derek frowned. "You mean we're staying at a hotel, right?"

Gwen adjusted the strap on her shoulder. "No. A hostel."

He arched a brow. "Aren't hostels like boarding houses?"

"Yes," Gwen replied as she started walking down the concourse. The others fell into step with her.

"Believe me, the hostel we're staying at is a palace compared to the accommodations we'll have in Moswani," Joyce commented.

Gwen noticed the brief hesitation in

Derek's eyes. "Where do we stay?" he asked.

"If you'd made the meetings you'd know we're staying in an abandoned hospital," Gwen said over her shoulder.

"Point taken."

She slowed and glanced at him to see if her censure had offended him.

He shrugged, clearly not offended. "This will be an adventure I'm sure to remember."

For some reason his dismissive attitude grated on Gwen's nerves. She reminded herself of his father's wish for Derek to see the part of their mission that went beyond just the obvious. "This isn't a vacation. We'll be doing a great deal of good for the people of Moswani. They are the ones to remember."

Derek gave her a "what's your problem" look. "Good to know."

"Don't mind her. She's all work and no play," Joyce said with a teasing lilt to her voice.

A good dose of irritation shot through Gwen's veins. Just because she took life seriously didn't mean she didn't know how to relax and have fun. She'd enjoyed swimming in the ocean the few times she had gone to the coast along the Oregon and Washington border.

She liked to go to concerts and hear jazz or Christian artists. She'd gone to every one of her friend Tyler's basketball games. Though she had to have the game explained to her. But still, she'd had fun.

Only, looking into Derek's amused eyes, she realized their concept of relaxing fun would be vastly different. He'd be off running himself to the max. Or out partying. She'd heard from the nurses that he did the nightclub scene in Seattle.

So what did it matter if they didn't share mutual downtime pursuits? What mattered was the work they'd be doing in Africa. Not filling his adventure scrapbook.

One more hurdle to cross to fulfilling her promise.

Chapter Two

Gwen picked up her pace, wanting a breather from her companions. The concourse seemed a mile long and lined with more shops that any airport she'd ever been in. The typical tourist-type stores with hats and T-shirts blazing with the red, white and blue flag of Britain. Stores selling designer clothes, which no doubt cost more than Gwen made in a year.

Coming into the main terminal, she headed for the Tube station, since their baggage was checked all the way through to Uganda and would be there when they arrived. Unlike the subway of New York, the station was shiny silver with the longest escalator she'd ever seen.

They boarded the Tube. The eclectic assortment of passengers showed little interest in the Americans boarding.

Joyce, Craig and Ned took a row of seats beside a sullen teenage boy dressed in black. Gwen chose to stand and Derek halted next to her, his big hand wrapping around the overhead bar just millimeters from her own.

The Tube shot forward. Gwen braced her feet apart to keep her balance. Outside the window the dimly lit walls of the tunnels whooshed by in a blur. Gwen turned her gaze away because she'd learned the last time she rode on the Tube that watching out the window made her motion sickness kick in.

Derek captured her gaze and smiled. "So is that true?"

"What?" Gwen tried not to let his nearness and the killer smile have an effect on her. She told herself it was the excitement of the trip that sent her pulse pounding.

"That you're all work and no play?"

She lifted a corner of her mouth in a self-effacing smile. Now that she'd calmed down after Joyce's announcement, she decided she'd rather be a hard worker than a flake. "I suppose."

"What do you like to do for fun?" he asked, his green eyes alight with interest.

She shrugged. "Stuff."

"Like what?"

She thought about the question for a moment. "I like to walk on the beach. I read. I bike. Normal stuff."

"That's good. Are you a road bike or mountain bike person?"

She thought of the shiny blue metallic bike that Claire and Nick had given her when she'd moved to Seattle. "I have a road bike. To be honest, I haven't ridden in a long time. I tried to bike to work but it didn't work out. You know Seattle. Too many hills."

"Very true. What kind of books?"

"For fun?"

He nodded.

"I'm fascinated with historical fiction."

"I'm an action-adventure reader myself."

She laughed. "Why am I not surprised?"

The Tube slowed. A voice over the loud-speaker announced their arrival at Paddington Station.

"This is us," Gwen said.

Craig, Ned and Joyce rose from the bench and crowded toward the door. Gwen turned her back to Derek just as the car came to a jerking stop. The force of the train's abrupt halt caused several people to stumble. Someone bumped into Gwen, knocking her off balance. Derek's arm coiled around her, steadying her.

Her already parched mouth went impossibly drier at the contact. She gathered her bearings and stepped away from him with a slight shiver. "Thank you, again."

He grinned and winked. "Anytime."

The doors opened and they stepped out into the brisk evening air. The tree-lined streets bustled with activity. There were black cabs, double-decker red buses and cars going by with nobody in the driver's seat.

The facades of the buildings retained their time-gone-by feel that made Gwen smile. She loved the grand feel of London and the history represented in the architecture. The arched doorways and colorful doors of the tall slim houses that were built together as if sharing the walls, called to her. Someday she'd like to live in London.

Their hostel was two blocks down on the right. The two-story yellow brick building sat in the middle of the block. An archway over a red door welcomed them. Arched windows with wrought iron balconies gave the building charm.

The proprietor, who introduced himself as Damon, greeted them warmly and showed them to their accommodations. They passed a room with comfy-looking couches that served as the common area, then up a narrow staircase with an ornately carved banister.

The wood floors of the hallway were covered with worn blue runners. Gwen was thankful they each had separate rooms with a single bathroom just down the hall.

The rooms weren't fancy, but they were clean and functional with a single bed, scratched-up dresser and small closet with empty hangers. Gwen's room shared a wall with Joyce's while the men's rooms were across the way.

Derek and the others were making plans for a late dinner. Gwen listened for a moment before stepping into her room and closing the door. Her plan was to relax and prepare for the rest of the journey; the long flight in the morning from the UK to Africa, then the drive from Entebbe Airport to the Moswani province.

To that end, she grabbed a few toiletries and stepped back into the hall which was thankfully empty. She wasn't big on small talk.

Between the long flight and the eight-hour time difference, she felt ready to grab a bite to eat at the little pub next door and then sleep. Refreshed, she opened the bathroom door and found Derek leaning against the wall.

She blinked. "Uh, it's all yours."

"Is there any hot water left?" he asked.

She bit her lip. "I think so. I wasn't in there that long."

His mouth quirked. "I'm teasing."

"Oh." She didn't know him well enough to recognize when he was teasing or not. "I hope you're not too uncomfortable with the accommodations here."

He waved off her concern. "I lived in a dorm in college."

"Well, Joyce wasn't kidding when she said this is luxurious compared to where we'll be staying next."

He lightly tweaked her braid. "Don't worry about me. I'm adaptable."

She stepped away from him. "That's good. I'll see you in the morning."

"Hey, wait," he said. "We're all going to dinner in an hour. You're coming, too."

She cocked her head, not liking the way he told her what she was doing. "I don't think so."

"You have to eat. And from what the others were telling me, this might be the last normal meal we'll get until we're back here."

"I don't want to stay out late."

The excuse was lame. She had no real reason not to join them other than she just wasn't good in casual settings. She didn't do the chitchatty, surface deal that Joyce was so good at. She hadn't learned the fine art of conversation. Living on the street, it wasn't a priority—wondering where the next meal was coming from was. She gave another prayer of thanks for Claire and the teen shelter she'd created, which helped get her off the street.

"I promise I won't keep you out long." He stepped into the bathroom. "I'll come get you in an hour." With that he shut the door.

Gwen frowned. He was awfully pushy, but she couldn't deny that eating alone as usual wasn't appealing. Maybe it was time to step out of her comfort zone and try to have a casual dinner out with the team.

Her team.

She had to keep reminding herself that she was in charge and responsible for the success of the mission and the safety of the people. A heavy load, but one she willingly bore.

An hour later, there was a knock on the door to her room. Her heart leaped and she forced herself to stay calm. This wasn't a date. She wouldn't be alone with Derek. Still she smoothed a hand over the skirt she'd brought to wear to church in the village.

She opened the door expecting to see Derek and found only Craig and Joyce standing in the hall.

Disappointment spiraled through Gwen and she forced the silly emotion down. She had no business caring one way or another about Derek's whereabouts.

Still the anxious flutter of nerves warned her that she wasn't as unaffected by him as she wanted to be. Not good. Not good at all.

Gwen forced a smile and stepped into the hall. "Hi, guys. Where are the other two?"

"Ned and Derek went on ahead to secure a table," Joyce explained as they headed down the stairs.

"Boy, I'm starved." Craig held open the door for the ladies. Gwen smiled at him

as she left the hostel, liking his gentle-
manly manners.

Joyce had changed into a pair of linen
pants and a bright pink tank top that
showed off her creamy complexion. Her
dark hair curled in appealing ringlets.
Craig had shaved, his young face looking
even more boyish. His jeans and polo shirt
could have used an iron.

They walked two blocks to a quaint restaurant called Monica's. The entryway
boasted dark mahogany wood and antique
furnishings. Waiters with white aprons
hustled about. Tantalizing aromas hung in
the air and Gwen's stomach rumbled.

At a white linen-covered table near the
back Derek waved them over. He looked
good, with his freshly washed hair and
clean-shaven face, though there was
nothing boyish about Derek. His broad
shoulders filled out his silk blue shirt. He
looked solid and sturdy. The type who
liked to be in control.

Gwen hung back slightly, unsure where
to sit.

Derek stood and pulled out a chair for Joyce and then turned to her. "Here you go." He pulled out the chair next to where he'd been sitting.

"Thanks," she murmured as she sat. Awareness tingled over her arms. She shivered.

He folded himself back into his chair. "Cold?"

She shook her head and picked up the menu. Traditional British Cuisine the top read. "This is an interesting place. How did you find it?"

Derek picked up his own menu. "Damon suggested it."

"Get a load of this food," Craig commented.

The one-page menu didn't offer a great deal of choice but each dish listed was described in captivating detail, complete with its particular historical background. Gwen put her menu down. She swallowed a lump of dread. Nothing on the menu was traditional for her.

"Ooo. Calf's liver and beetroot. Yum,"

Joyce said with a wince that indicated she thought the dish anything but appealing.

A young woman approached their table. Her short spiked hair was tipped blue and one earring dangled from her right earlobe. "Ready to order?" she asked, her accent making it clear she was a local.

Each member of the team ordered something different from the traditional menu.

Then it was Gwen's turn. She could feel the attention on her. "Do you have just fish and chips?"

The waitress sighed. "Yes."

"Oh, come on. Try the Arbroath Smokie with me," Derek said, his green eyes steady on her. "It's haddock, smoked over an open fire. You'd like it."

She frowned at the description. "No, I wouldn't."

To the waitress, she stated firmly, "The fish and chips, please."

Better to go with something she'd had before than risk ordering something that she couldn't eat and wasting the food.

Once the girl left, the conversation

flowed easily enough. First with mundane get-to-know-you type things. Education, home towns and hobbies. Gwen participated a little, giving short evasive answers that made her sound an awful lot like Ned. She almost giggled, but managed to rein her amusement in.

But the small talk was wearing.

Soon the conversation turned to politics and became more animated as they discussed state issues and abuse of natural resources in the Pacific Northwest. Their food arrived and the conversation died down as they all concentrated on their meals.

"Here, try this," Derek said as he offered her a forkful of his haddock.

She wrinkled her nose. "No. Too fishy." Using the excuse of the fish, she backed away from the intimacy of his offering her food from his plate.

"How can you say that without tasting it?"

"I can smell it."

"Be adventurous. Just taste it."

"I *am* adventurous. You stop being so

pushy." She glared at him, but found it hard to be mad when his green eyes sparkled with amusement as he ate the bite intended for her.

When they left the restaurant, Joyce said she wanted to see some sights. Craig and Ned said they'd go, as well.

"Count me in," Derek said. "Gwen?"

She shook her head. "I need to sleep."

"Thought you said you were adventurous?"

There was challenge in his tone and she chafed against the need to prove to him that she could be adventurous. "We all should rest for the trip."

"We can rest on the plane," Derek replied. "We won't stay out too late. Come on. How often do you get to just play?"

She felt torn between what she thought she should do and what she really wanted to do. She wanted to go, to be a part of the group, and see London at night.

To play.

But wouldn't the more responsible, practical course be to turn in?

Of course, this could be a perfect opportunity to talk to Derek about how the group provides healing in so many ways beyond just the physical. So much was riding on this mission. She wanted to make Doc Harper proud and fulfill his wishes. She wanted to be a good leader.

"All right. Let's go."

The group set out. Ned, Craig and Joyce led the way while Derek walked along with Gwen. She and Derek lagged slightly behind the others. She found herself relaxing and enjoying his lively humor as she took in the sights—the spectacular Tower Bridge spanning the Thames, the Houses of Parliament and Big Ben.

His stories of growing up on Bainbridge Island, where his parents still resided enthralled her. It sounded so *Leave it to Beaver*-ish. So far removed from her own experiences as a homeless teen.

"Someone in the office said you're a world-class marathon runner."

He shrugged. "I've had some success."

She waited, expecting him to expound

on his successes. He didn't. She liked that. She forced herself to remember why she hadn't returned to the hostel. "The place we are going in Africa is very far removed from the rest of the world. You hear so much about AIDS in Africa, but malaria cases are more rampant worldwide. For many, Hands of Healing is the only hope of medical care they have."

"You don't have to sell me on the importance of why we're going," he stated softly.

No, she supposed she didn't. He was his father's son after all, but then why did Dr. Harper feel it necessary to ask her to promise to try to make Derek see that the healing they brought went beyond the physical? Shouldn't Derek already know that?

"Tell me more about you," he said.

"Not much to tell. Born in Portland, Oregon. Went to med school at OSHU in Portland. Pretty boring really," she said, hoping he wouldn't push for more details.

She didn't share the pain of her childhood with anyone, let alone a man who had a perfect upbringing with loving parents. He wouldn't understand.

The group stopped in front of a large cathedral. The spire rose heavenward and was lit from within. The big stone structure made Gwen feel small and insignificant against the history and power of faith that the building represented.

"We should get back before we all turn into pumpkins," Joyce announced on a yawn.

Everyone agreed and returned to the hostel. As late as it was, Gwen didn't feel exhausted or tired. She could have stayed out all night and been fine. The time spent with Derek and the others had been unexpectedly fun.

In the hall to their rooms they said goodnight. Craig and Ned disappeared inside their rooms. Joyce lingered a moment then she, too, went inside her room, leaving Gwen and Derek alone in the hall.

"See, that wasn't so bad," Derek teased.

She smiled. "It was nice to 'play.' Thanks for talking me into going with you guys."

He shrugged. "'All work and no play,' as they say."

Remembering Joyce's earlier comment, Gwen impulsively asked, "Do you find me dull?"

His gaze touched her face and lingered on her lips. "Not all at. I find you fascinating."

She swallowed the unexpected lump in her throat. "You do?"

He nodded.

Had he moved closer? Against logic, against her ingrained sense of self-preservation, she swayed slightly toward him as if some invisible force was pulling her forward. Her gaze took in his features, memorizing the angle of his nose, the planes of his cheekbones. The fullness of his lips.

He gave her a crooked grin as his head dipped. She steadied herself, waiting, wondering, and fought the need to run, to protect herself.

Her eyes closed and her hands fisted in an effort to stay put. The air felt heavy as he came closer. Her breath hitched as old fears and unwanted memories battered at her consciousness.

His lips gently pressed against her forehead.

Her eyelids jerked open as confusion and then disappointment rushed in, filling her lungs to bursting.

"Good night, Gwen. I'll see you in the morning," he said before he turned and went into his own room.

She blinked. She put her hand to her hot cheeks.

What just happened?

For a brief moment she'd wanted him to kiss her. And he had. Only not in the way she'd expected.

Dope! Where would a kiss have led anyway?

Nowhere that she intended to go. That was for sure.

Becoming involved with her boss's son was not something she was going to let happen.

Period.

End of story.

She fled to the sanctuary of her little room, wondering why she felt so let down. By him or herself?

Chapter Three

The next morning Gwen awoke groggy from too little deep sleep. She didn't regret spending the time the night before with the others. The bonding could only be good for the team.

She tried to analyze her feelings for Derek. He confused her and intrigued her. He obviously was ambitious and driven, yet there was a wildness in him that kept her on edge.

She had to keep a tight grip on the magnetic pull he had on her. Yes, he was good-looking. But more than that, something about him called to a restlessness inside her that she refused to unleash.

Best to keep a strictly professional demeanor around him and not form any sort of attachment.

With that settled in her mind, she dressed in black, stretchy yoga pants and a bright pink, long, lace-edged tunic T-shirt, then packed up and went to join the group in the common room where they were munching on scrambled eggs and toast. She immediately noticed Derek's absence.

"Where's Derek?"

Craig, sitting on the couch drinking from a water bottle, shrugged. He'd shaved and his dark hair was pulled back into its customary ponytail. His cargo pants and rust-colored Henley shirt made him look as though he was ready to go skateboarding rather than head to Africa.

"Took a run. Now showering," Ned replied before stuffing his mouth with a bite of toast. He wore Bermuda shorts and a solid orange, short-sleeved button-down shirt. The outfit suggested he was a vacationer ready to go sightseeing, not travel halfway around the globe to help those less fortunate than himself.

Joyce dipped a tea bag in hot water. Her apparel was much more understated—dark jeans and a striped T-shirt. Her dark curls were stuffed under her hat. She'd applied a touch of makeup to accentuate her classical bone structure and wide eyes. "I wish I'd known he was going for a run. I'd have joined him."

An unfamiliar sensation slid down Gwen's spine. She frowned and shook it off before pouring some hot water from a silver pot into a flowered china cup. Whatever developed between Joyce and Derek was none of her business. Her only concern was to make sure he understood the work and came away appreciating the importance of what they did.

"I hope he's ready soon," she said to no one in particular.

"You don't have to worry about me."

Gwen's whole being went on alert. She slowly pivoted and watched Derek come into the room wearing flat-front khaki shorts and a white, short-sleeved shirt hanging open over a print screen T-shirt of a basketball player making a jump shot. He exuded confidence and health. With his smooth square jaw and freshly blow-dried hair, he could easily be a model for some sports and fitness magazine.

Gwen forced her gaze from his long muscular legs to his eyes which glinted with a knowing amusement. As if he'd sensed her attraction before she had even become aware of it.

"Good," she said in a decisive tone that hid the pounding of her heart—far from a "professional" reaction to the man.

Derek gave her a short nod as he moved past her to the table where the food had been set out. He put a piece of toast on a plate and then poured himself a cup of coffee.

Gwen drank her tea while the group chatted and finished up their breakfast. After paying for their stay they were off to Heathrow. Though Derek was considerate and charming, Gwen sensed a distance that hadn't been there the night before. He didn't tease her or flash his grin at all.

She should be thankful.

Really, she should.

As she settled into a seat in the waiting area at the gate, she wondered if she'd done something to offend him. She silenced a groan. Maybe she'd seemed too forward or willing to be kissed last night and that had repulsed him. Maybe he did find her dull even though he'd claimed the opposite.

She gave a sharp shake of her head as old echoes of worthlessness tried to rise. No. She was a strong independent woman who didn't need validation from anyone, let alone a man she barely knew.

Over the years, guarding her heart and her space had become as natural as breathing.

If she stayed prepared and in control, she'd never have to be vulnerable again.

Derek leaned against a concrete pillar while the rest of the group sat in the stiff black chairs in the wide waiting area of the airline's boarding gate. He didn't see why they'd want to sit now when they'd be sitting for the next eight or so hours in the confining plane cabin.

He longed to get out and run off more of the relentless energy that buzzed through his system. The sprint from the morning had barely assuaged his need to move. He'd been keyed up ever since he'd almost kissed Gwen the night before.

Man, what had he been thinking?

At least he'd had the good sense to divert his mouth to the petal softness of her forehead and not touched the apricot-colored lips she'd offered. That would have been a huge mistake.

He acknowledged he was commitment-phobic. He'd certainly heard it from every female in his life, including his mother. He accepted he was a love-'em-and-leave-'em kind of guy. It worked for him.

Gwen was not a love-'em-and-leave-'em kind of woman.

And if he did anything to hurt her, his

father would skin him alive. Not what he was going for.

He had to stay focused. Life was an adventure that he fully intended to live.

Without the burden of a relationship.

He prayed, something he didn't do often, that he'd find the will to keep from acting on the attraction sizzling between them.

Gwen decided not to spend any more time worrying about Derek and his mood. She'd had enough of that growing up, trying to determine when she was safe and when she should hide. She'd vowed never to be at the mercy of someone else again.

Their flight would be taking off soon. Once they reached their destination, she'd fulfill her promise to her mentor and focus her energy on making this mission a success. Though her definition of success wouldn't match that of world opinion.

Success meant knowing she'd made a difference in the world, demonstrated God's love in a real and tangible way.

"Hey, guys, let's pray before we board," she said to the group.

"Good idea." Joyce stood. Craig and Ned followed suit. Gwen rose, took Joyce's hand in her left hand and then waved Derek over with her right hand.

He pushed off the pillar and slowly made his way to join their circle. He frowned as his gaze took in their linked hands. "What's this?"

Gwen pinned him with her gaze. "We're going to say a prayer for a safe journey."

"Can't we each silently say our own prayer?"

Was Dr. Harper wrong about his son's faith? He'd said Derek had accepted Christ as his Savior as a teen, but that didn't necessarily make him a believer.

"'For where two or three are gathered,'" Gwen quoted Matthew 18:20 softly, then narrowed her gaze. "What's the problem?"

Derek glanced around. "I just don't think we need to advertise."

"Uh-oh," murmured Joyce. She and Ned exchanged a knowing glance.

Fire erupted in Gwen's belly. She raised her brows. "Excuse me?"

"This whole 'public prayer' thing makes us look like religious fanatics," he said.

There was a challenge in his eyes that grated on her nerves. When it came to the faith that had saved her life, she didn't cut any slack.

She dropped Joyce's hand and moved in front of him. "Would you rather we slinked off to some dark corner to pray? Are you that ashamed of your faith?"

His eyebrows drew together. "I'm not ashamed. I just don't like public prayer."

"Because of what other people, people you don't know or have any relationship with, will think?"

"I don't think it's a good witness to nonbelievers to appear like fanatics."

She dropped her chin, remembering the way Claire and her aunt Denise had worn their faith out in the open and had taught Gwen the power of faith. She'd not understood at first. In fact, she'd thought the two women were out to lunch for sure.

Slowly, with time and patience, they'd softened her heart.

Claire had done that not only for her, but for a myriad of other teens with her teen shelter. Teens like Tyler. He wasn't Gwen's brother but if she had to have one, she'd choose him. He started out rough and pure rebel, but now he'd made them all proud by graduating from college. Unlike Derek, Tyler would never shrink from showing his faith.

She struggled to contain her temper. "So it's a better witness to hide our faith? Like we're doing something wrong and shameful? That doesn't make sense." Shaking her head, she stepped away. "You can pray with us or not. Free will, that's what it's called."

Retaking Joyce's hand, she then reached over to take Ned's, closing Derek out of the circle. "Craig, would you, please?"

Craig's stunned expression cleared and he nodded. "Sure. Dear Father in heaven, we ask for a safe journey to our destination…"

Gwen tried to concentrate on the prayer and agreed with Craig's softly spoken words in her heart, but she was too aware of Derek standing just a few feet behind her. His presence like a menacing cloud.

Dear Lord, she silently prayed, *soften his heart.*

How was she going to show him the true good that Hands of Healing International did if he couldn't even demonstrate his faith in public?

Derek felt like an idiot as he stood alone outside the prayer circle. He hadn't meant to make such a big deal about the prayer.

He'd never been comfortable with public worship. Maybe it was pride. Or that to him communing with God seemed such a personal thing, reserved for special occasions.

He didn't get the whole God and man relationship jargon his father and mother preached. How could he have a relationship with Someone who wasn't there, at least physically?

He'd read parts of the Bible, understood the basic fundamentals. The Ten Commandments sounded like a good idea. If everyone followed them, there'd sure be less crime and destruction in the world. He did get that God loved him, but he'd never felt that love. Not like his dad apparently did.

As he watched his four travel companions, their heads bowed and their hands linked, he suddenly had the strongest yearning to be included.

Strange, since he wasn't much of a team player. He liked working and competing alone.

But he'd signed on to be a part of this team. Time to act like a team player and honor the bond started the night before.

He forced himself not to glance around to see how the general populace was reacting to his companions' public display. Moving to stand between Gwen and Ned, he slipped his hands between theirs.

Gwen's delicate hand fit perfectly against his palm.

A little too perfectly for comfort.

She started, her amber gaze surprised, then pleased. Ned winked at him before returning to a humble posture of prayer. Derek closed his eyes and let the rest of Craig's prayer wash over him.

"…we ask for guidance and wisdom as we work together as a team to provide care to those in need. We thank You for this opportunity, Lord. In Jesus's name, amen."

"Amen," Derek murmured.

Gwen squeezed his hand before abruptly letting go. A warmth spread through him. Oh, boy, he would be in trouble if her approval started to mean something to him.

No way was he letting himself go down that treacherous path. Approval was one step away from commitment. He never wanted to be in a position where he could disappoint anyone.

From now on, keeping his distance from the pretty redhead was priority number one.

Derek decided to walk off the sudden buzz of energy making his muscles ache. He needed another hard run. He wasn't looking forward to being cooped up on a second long flight.

"Mind if I walk with you?" Craig asked as he fell into step with Derek.

"Not at all." They walked at a steady pace down the concourse. "How many trips have you been on now?"

"This is my first with Hands of Healing. I spent the summer between high school and college in Mexico building houses with another organization."

"Then you and I will both get to see what this is all about."

Craig nodded. "I was looking forward to learning from your father."

"Yeah, me, too." Disappointment was a bitter pill he'd long ago learned to swallow when it came to his father.

"But Joyce says Gwen's great and will have everything running smoothly."

"No doubt." He glanced back toward where Gwen and the others were seated.

Gwen struck him as super-detailed and organized. More than just her hair was braided tight. But he liked that she didn't need gobs of makeup or flashy jewelry to draw attention to herself. She had a natural beauty that the touch of lip gloss she wore complimented rather than distracted from, as it seemed to on other women.

Craig stopped to admire a flashy BMW coupe on display in the middle of the terminal. He whistled through his teeth as he inspected the sticker on the window. "These things are steep."

Derek nodded, thinking about his own little sports car at home sitting securely in his garage. He'd bought the car with the money from his first endorsement check. He'd been so anxious to show it off to his father.

Dad had admired the car and congratulated him, but had declined a spin in the fancy ride because, as always, he had to get back to the clinic.

Always the clinic.

Derek had spent his whole life competing against the clinic for his dad's attention. Maturity had taught him he would never win that race. Now, as CEO of Hands of

Healing International, Derek hoped to share a common bond with his dad.

An overhead speaker announced that their flight would soon be boarding. They rejoined their group, boarded the plane and soon were taxiing down the runway. Derek settled back in his first-class seat, mentally preparing himself for the long journey ahead and for dealing with Gwen's distracting presence.

The plane touched down without a hitch on the tarmac of Entebbe airport in Uganda. The darkness of night kept Derek from seeing much outside the windows of the plane as he stood, his muscles waking up from the long period of inactivity, and moved toward the staircase.

This would be his first time on the continent of Africa. He'd traveled most of Europe, the Caribbean, North and South America, and parts of Asia. He looked forward to this experience.

The minute he stepped out on the landing a chill swept through him. He remembered someone saying the nights were cold and the days hot. At the moment he'd have welcomed the sun.

Walking down the portable stairs he tried to adjust to the strange scent of Africa: diesel, dirt and something unfamiliar. The heaviness in the air put pressure on his lungs. Drawing in a complete breath proved difficult. He could only hope that once away from the city the air would be fresh, less constricting.

He stepped onto the tarmac and moved aside to wait for the others. They trickled off the plane, looking tired and moving slowly.

Only Gwen seemed to have any energy. "We all here?"

Wondering where she stored such perkiness, Derek nodded. "What now?"

"This way."

She glided across the tarmac, the others trailing along behind her, toward the building Derek assumed was the terminal. He ruefully shook his head. Looked as if Gwen was taking charge now. Just as long as she didn't try to take charge of him.

The end of the building that faced the tarmac had a huge roll-up door that stood open to reveal the stark tile-and-concrete interior. Before entering the building they had to stop at the tall tables manned by uniformed airport personnel.

After presenting their paperwork and having their passports stamped, they were permitted to enter. Derek noticed several armed military men patrolling the perimeter of the building. He wasn't sure if he felt secure or threatened by the show of force.

Up ahead, Gwen conversed with an African man roughly her own height, dressed in a bright yellow shirt and tan slacks. His smooth skin betrayed no hint of age. However, the concern on his face mirrored the expressions on Joyce's, Ned's and Craig's faces.

"I'm not worried about that," Gwen said, though her brow furrowed slightly.

"I want to make sure you are aware of the situation," the African responded, his accented voice flowing evenly.

"Guys?" Gwen's question included them all.

"What did I miss?" Derek asked.

Gwen turned to him. "This is Moses, our contact with Family in Crisis. Moses, this is Derek Harper."

Derek held out his hand. "Nice to meet you."

Moses's grip was strong. "Welcome. We are sad to hear that your father hurt himself."

"He was explaining that the Kony Rebels have moved into the province of Moswani. They want to liberate it from the Ugandan government," Gwen explained.

That didn't sound good. "Which means...?"

"It means we have to be careful and stick close to the clinic. War is a part of life in Africa. So, I say we go on with our mission and trust that God will protect us."

"I don't plan on getting on another plane for two weeks," Joyce commented with a bit of defiance in her tone.

"We stay. We're needed," came Ned's reply.

Craig shrugged. "I'm game."

Derek didn't know how this new development would affect his agenda, but if the others were staying… "I'm in."

Gwen gave a short nod. "All right, then."

"Come, we gather your bags." Moses led the way to the baggage claim area where they met up with another African.

"Hey, Ethan." Ned shook the newcomer's hand.

"Glad to see you back in my country." Ethan's deep baritone voice reverberated through the group.

Derek was introduced and immediately liked Ethan. There was something soothing about the man's demeanor. Though not as tall as Moses, Ethan had a commanding presence.

His dark hands were crisscrossed with small scars and one jagged scar slashed over his neck and disappeared into the collar of his shirt. Derek couldn't begin to imagine how different these men's lives were from his own.

They all helped to load the bags of supplies they'd shipped into the back of a dusty white minivan before piling inside. It was a tight fit and not everyone had a seat belt.

Derek squeezed by the window in the back with Craig and Ned beside him. Gwen sat directly in front of him. Her long braid hung over the back of her seat.

She pointed toward a building they were passing that he could barely make out. "That's the original airport. The site of the raid on Entebbe in '76."

All he could think to say was "Ah."

He'd been a kid when the hijacking occurred. He remembered being thankful his father had been home and not off trying to save the world that fall. The coverage on TV had seemed overwhelming at the time.

The minivan soon left the airport behind. Driving on what seemed to be the wrong side of the road, they drove through Kampala, the capital of Uganda. There was a noticeable lack of streetlights on the still-active streets. Tall buildings rose to obscure the skyline.

Once out of the city, the darkness closed

in. The headlights showed little of the countryside. They bumped along on uneven pavement, stopped at the check-points where armed guards inspected Moses's papers and flashed bright lights into the van. They were waved on.

Eventually the pavement turned into a dirt road that they traveled down for several hours before stopping in front of a dark squat structure, unlit and forbidding.

They climbed out. Dust rose, choking in swirling gusts as the group moved about unloading the van. Derek looked around. Not much to see at night. The outline of trees and in the distance other dark structures.

The air was still heavy but the smell of diesel had lessened, accentuating the strange smell he'd noticed earlier. Joyce hadn't been kidding when she'd said the hostel was a palace compared to here.

"What is that smell?" Derek whispered to Craig.

"Probably charcoal."

"Charcoal?"

"It's the fuel they use to cook with," Craig replied.

Derek took in the sight of the destination. There were no streetlights or even a porch light offering welcome.

He followed the others inside, which was no better than the outside. A few bare bulbs dimly lit the interior. The front door opened to a big room. The concrete floor and walls made him feel boxed in.

"This way." Ned nudged him forward as he passed by carrying a heavy-duty flashlight.

Derek followed down a narrow, unlit hallway. They turned right into an enormous room with several bunk beds. Ned deposited his pack on the mattress of the nearest bottom bunk.

"Take your pick," he said with a tired grin.

Derek put his stuff on a nearby bottom mattress and realized with dread that the mattress was really just a chunk of foam. Good thing he liked to camp.

"Restroom?" he asked Ned just as Craig walked in.

The other two men exchanged a glance and then chuckled softly.

Craig threw his pack on the top bunk over Ned. "Come on. I'll show you out back. The outhouse is not as deluxe as the typical portable restroom."

"Great," Derek said without enthusiasm. He followed Craig back down the hall and outside. Gwen was talking with Ethan and Moses. When she saw him, she came over.

"You okay?" she asked, worry softening her gaze.

"Dandy," he muttered, uncomfortable with the way her concern warmed him.

She laughed. "You'll do fine. I'll see you in the morning. That's when the real fun begins."

He reached out to finger her silky braid. "How on earth can you be so chipper?"

"Working on adrenaline here."

"I didn't realize it would be so…rustic."

She gave him a soft smile. "This is paradise compared to some of the places I've been."

His brows drew together in confusion. "What?"

Reaching up to remove his hand, she said, "Good night."

He watched her walk inside. At times she seemed so buttoned-up and reserved. Yet, he'd seen glimpses of a softer side. A side that told him she was a woman with a great capacity to love.

A very interesting woman. He reminded himself he didn't want to be interested.

Chapter Four

Gwen woke as the first rooster crowed. Through the small, square window in the room the sun was barely visible on the horizon. She heard movement in the building, the others already working. There was so much preparation to do before the villagers began to arrive.

She'd planned on waking earlier, but since she hadn't been able to rest on the flight, she'd fallen into an exhausted, deep sleep as soon as she'd hit the foam mattress.

She blamed Derek for her inability to relax on the flight from the UK. Every time she'd close her eyes and start to doze off, she'd jerk awake expecting to find Derek standing in the aisle watching her again.

And every time she experienced a burst of disappointment when he wasn't there.

Talk about unnerving.

Careful not to disturb a still-sleeping Joyce, she quickly dressed in faded jeans, a plain green T-shirt and her hiking boots. Nothing better than good footwear, regardless of the weather.

She savored the slight chill in the air because in a few hours the sun would rise fully, and this close to the equator the heat would be intense. She quickly lathered on sunscreen where her limbs were exposed. Unfolding a wide-brimmed cotton hat from her pack, she headed toward the room that they would be using as the main treatment room of the clinic.

Moses, Ethan and Ned were already setting up.

"Good morning, gentlemen," she said. "Are Craig and Derek still sleeping?"

Ned shook his head. "Haven't seen Derek. Craig's checking on breakfast."

"Okay," she replied.

Today she'd let Derek and Joyce sleep in, but starting tomorrow they all would start early. She began unloading boxes of gauze, syringes, alcohol swabs, bandages and various other products they might need to treat a mixture of symptoms and conditions that could arise from the living conditions and lack of resources available to this part of the world.

She directed the men where to arrange the long tables they'd acquired from a nearby school. This particular building had been built with the sole purpose of medical treatment.

Unfortunately, the charitable group that had erected the structure had had to leave due to financial constraints, abandoning the building.

Dr. Harper had bought the building and wanted to provide continuous care, but finding staff to stay for more than a few weeks at a time had proved difficult. He allowed other charitable organizations use of the facility whenever possible.

Gwen set up the clinic the way Dr. Harper had taught her, placing an administrative desk near the door where the patients would check in before coming to see Gwen who would determine the nature of their illness. Depending on the complaint, the patients would be funneled to either Joyce, if the patient was a child or teen, or Craig, for adults with non-life threatening ailments. Ned would do any sort of surgical procedures that didn't require more than localized anesthesia.

Joyce wandered out of the back room, looking groggy in her cotton drawstring cropped pants and pullover shirt. Her short dark curls stuck out in all directions. "Coffee?"

"Go see Craig in the kitchen," Gwen replied, hoping Craig had found the supply of coffee in the food bag they'd brought and set a pot to brewing.

Derek came out a short while later, dressed in lightweight running shorts, a white T-shirt with a sport logo emblazoned across the front and worn running shoes. His wiry, muscled legs and lean torso showed the effects of his training. He looked every inch the runner, not someone ready to help with a medical clinic.

Gwen narrowed her gaze. Using her best Sunday school teacher voice, she said, "Hey, Harper. We could use your help here."

Appearing not the least repentant, he shrugged. "Sure. What are we doing?"

She explained the logistics of the clinic, stressing the humanitarian aspects whenever possible, and directed him to help Moses stack the appropriate supplies in the right places.

Craig came through the front door. He grinned as he said, "Breakfast, anyone?"

They all filed out of the clinic. Children of various ages and sizes ran about. Several sat in the dirt eating with their fingers from bowls of porridge or Matoke. Smiling faces, but their potbellies showed they were malnourished. Gwen's heart squeezed. She knew many would never reach adulthood and for those that did, few would live to be old and gray.

"Wow, I didn't expect all these kids," Derek commented as he dodged a running child.

"Most of these children are orphans living with either family members or with other families who've taken them in," Joyce explained.

"Why so many orphans?" Derek asked, his gaze meeting Gwen's.

She replied, "Between illness, poor living conditions and war, many adults don't live very long."

"How many people live in these... houses?" he asked, indicating the many round, mud-sided huts.

"It depends. I've seen as many as twenty living together or as few as two or three," Gwen answered and noticed the pensive shadow in Derek's gaze.

They approached a small concrete-and-brick building with a corrugated tin roof. Smoke seeped from cracks in the bricks and out the windows. They stepped inside, blinking against the sting of smoke from the fire pits. Several village women sat on the dirt floor peeling and cutting green bananas.

A chorus of voices called out to them, *"Jambo!"*

At Derek's questioning glance she explained, "Swahili for 'hello, welcome.'"

"This is the kitchen?" Derek whispered in her ear, his lip twitching upward in a grimace.

Gwen remembered the same astonishment the first time she'd seen the open fires with the large black kettles suspended over the flames. The wood burned down to charcoal, which was reused. The whole scene was reminiscent of the 1800s. But this was modern compared to smaller, less Westernized villages in the bush.

They were served Matoke, steamed mashed bananas, in large clay bowls. Derek took a clay mug full of steaming coffee, as well.

Derek brought his bowl and sat down next to Gwen on a stone bench. All around them activity started as the villagers began to wander close, curious to see the foreigners. A layer of dirt covered everything. Low-lying palm trees and dense bushes surrounded the brick-and-mud shops and houses.

Men on bicycles rode by laden with sugarcane or bushels of bananas. Boda-boda—as the bicycle transportation was called—was the main means of travel besides walking in the bush. Gwen thought about donating her bicycle to the village when she returned home since she rarely used it.

Derek took a bite of his food. "This is interesting. Will this be breakfast every-day?"

"Probably," she replied, thinking how at one time in her life she'd have done just about anything for some food.

"Good thing I like bananas," he commented with a gleam in his green gaze, before taking another big bite.

"Food here is simple. Used for fuel, not comfort."

"Fuel is what I'll need." He finished off

his portion, set his bowl aside and wiped his mouth with a paper napkin. The playful light left his gaze. "Gwen, there's something we need to discuss."

Figuring he was concerned about his role in the clinic, she said, "Don't worry. I'm sure I'll have plenty to keep you busy."

"About that. I don't see what my presence here is going to accomplish. Without my dad here to shadow, I'm going to be in the way."

Secretly agreeing with that assessment, but remembering the promise she'd made and the enormity of his father's wish, she shook her head. "There's still plenty for you to learn. Even if you're only observing at times, you'll get a better understanding of the work and that understanding will help you when we get back to the States."

"True." His green eyes stared off in the distance.

She studied his profile. What could be going through his mind? He was a man used to being in charge, to running the show. To winning. Here, he was only to observe and help in minor ways. She couldn't imagine that would be easy for him.

Finally, he spoke. "I have to be straight with you, though. My dad and I had a deal."

A sensation of foreboding flashed across her skin. "A deal?"

He turned to look at her, his green eyes troubled but determined. "We…I have—"

"Hey, you two," Joyce called from the edge of the main building. "We have people already lining up. You want to come help?"

Gwen automatically stood, but the frustration in Derek's expression stopped her from moving. "Can we finish this tonight?"

He grinned but his gaze grew rueful. "Of course."

They started walking toward the clinic.

"I need to go for a run before the sun gets too high."

She stopped. "No."

He raised his brows. "Excuse me?"

"I know you're a runner and you like to keep in shape, but—"

He widened his stance, a determined

light in his gaze. "I won't be gone more than forty minutes."

"Fine. Run circles around the building if you want, but you're not leaving the village."

"Whoa. I know Dad put you in charge, but you're taking this a bit far."

Pulling in a deep breath and letting it out slowly, she tried to make him understand. "We are in the bush of Africa. You can't just go running off. It's too dangerous. You could get hurt."

A small, charming smile played at the corner of his mouth. "I didn't realize you cared, Yates."

She ignored the little bump in her heart rate his smile caused and glared at him. "You are my responsibility."

"I'm pretty sure I can take care of myself."

She rolled her eyes. "This isn't about your ego. This is about safety. Most Africans haven't seen a Caucasian before. If you go running through their front yards, they're going to freak out. Then there are the wild animals to consider and the civil war that's taking place."

"I thought you said you weren't worried about the civil war?"

She hated when her words came back to bite her. "I'm not. We have an emergency plan. Besides, I'm sure we're safe as long as we stay within the village and don't venture too close to the borders."

He shrugged. "I'll stay on the road. I need to keep up my training and that requires long-distance running to keep my heart as well as my muscles in shape."

She planted her fists on her hips. "No."

"I don't need your permission."

Men! Were they all so stubborn? Short of tying him down, she couldn't stop him. Her blood pounded behind her eyes. "Fine. Just let me find someone to go with you."

His dark blond brows drew together. "I don't need a babysitter."

No, he had her for that job. She made a face and stalked back to the clinic. A dozen people ranging in ages from a newborn infant to an elderly couple had already formed a line at the door. Her chest squeezed at the sight. She wanted to get on with the work, not deal with Derek Harper.

She found Moses, told him what she needed.

"I know just the person," he said and left the clinic.

Gwen went back outside. Derek stood under a yellow bark fever tree stretching. There was a tingling in the pit of her stomach as she watched his muscles bunch and flex. He really was a good-looking man, all lean and fit.

A few minutes later, Moses returned with a tall, lanky youth with solemn brown eyes. She guessed him to be around eighteen or nineteen at the most.

"This is Tito. He'll go with Dr. Harper's son," Moses said.

"Derek," Gwen called.

He jogged over, his eyes searching her face.

"Here's your escort. Tito," she said as she tried not to sink into Derek's gaze.

An amused glint reflected in the emerald of his eyes. "Great."

He turned to the boy and stuck out his hand. "Tito, I'm Derek."

They shook hands and then they set off, their long legs eating up the ground. One powerful man and one in training, striding through the dust of Africa. One light skinned, one dark skinned. Both very different, yet the same in God's eyes.

Gwen's heart thudded in her chest as she watched the two disappear into the bush.

Oh, Father, please bring them back safely.

She'd never forgive herself if something happened to Derek, and it had nothing to do with disappointing the good doctor.

"Moses, Tito isn't Ugandan, is he?"

"No. He is Kenyan."

"What's he doing here?" She started toward the clinic building.

"He came for the race."

Gwen froze. Distrust and dismay converged in her veins. "Race?"

Legs pumping and lungs expanding to draw a dusty breath, Derek pushed himself, forcing his muscles to feel the burn. Amazingly, Tito kept pace, his long, thin legs matching Derek stride for stride. Respect for the young man grew with each mile.

Side by side they ran down a level dirt path that cut through dense foliage. Palm trees shorter than the average man, bushes with big, deep green leaves and tall yellowing grass were a blur of color. The heat of the sun grew more intense with each fleeting moment. Tomorrow he'd have to start out earlier.

Clocking their progress with his runner's watch, Derek calculated the time into miles. They closed in on five miles relatively quickly. Not bad, considering he'd spent the last two days squashed in an airplane.

A mud-sided house with a thatched roof became visible in a clearing as the trail rounded a bend. In front of the dwelling stood a tall structure made of red bricks encased in mud and seeping with smoke. The shape of it reminded Derek of a beehive.

Nearby a child sat beneath a palm tree.

His little brown body was bare except for what amounted to a loincloth. He rose at the sight of them, his brown eyes wide, scared. *"Muzungu!"*

The boy bolted around the back of the house.

"What does that mean?" Derek asked as they left the place behind.

Tito flashed him a toothy grin. "White man."

Gwen's words rang through Derek's brain. *They see you running through their front yards, they'll freak out.*

Derek hadn't really thought that through. He'd traveled to a wide variety of places, mostly commercial and recreational spots, but he'd never been the minority before. It was a strange feeling to know his presence was viewed with fear. He didn't like it.

"Tito, what was that place?"

"Brick makers."

Interesting. He'd never given any thought to how bricks were made. Were they made the same way in America?

"We will go through here and head

back now," Tito said as he veered off the main path and onto a more narrow, hilly trail. They squeezed together, their steps nearly matching.

"You run well," Derek commented. The boy should be a professional.

"Thank you. You, too. For a *Muzungu*." Tito flashed his grin again.

"Yeah, well." Derek returned a grin. "Where are you from?" Tito seemed so much taller and leaner than the Ugandans he'd met.

"Kenya."

"What are you doing here?"

"Running."

Derek slanted him a glance. "You're in Uganda to run?"

Tito nodded.

"The marathon next week," Derek stated in comprehension. Little wonder the youth had no trouble with the grueling pace.

"I will win."

"You can dream," Derek shot back with a grin of his own.

Tito let loose a deep laugh.

The pace quickened slightly. Two runners vying for dominance, trying to outrun the other. Derek enjoyed the burst of adrenaline gushing through his veins.

Suddenly, Tito grabbed him by the arm and pulled him to an abrupt stop.

"What...?"

Then Derek saw why they'd stopped. Up ahead, a large, black monkey stood in the middle of the path on all fours. Derek blinked. His heart thudded as his adrenaline rush turned to fear. Every instinct screamed turn and run. He prepared his body to do just that.

"Stay," Tito hissed from the side of his mouth.

The monkey rose to its hind feet and spread its arms wide, making itself look bigger. As if it could scare Derek more than it already did. Black eyes stared at them daring them to challenge him for dominance.

The animal bared its yellowed, sharp teeth and a low rumble emanated from its massive chest. The birds in the trees silenced and the very air seemed to still as if the world understood the dangers of this creature.

Movement from the bushes drew Derek's attention. More monkeys appeared, smaller versions of the bigger one. Their eyes darted toward the intruders.

Unlike the big one, these didn't bare their teeth or show any challenging actions. They darted across the path behind their menacing guardian and vanished into the thick underbrush.

As soon as the last one disappeared, the big one dropped back to all fours and hurried after the others.

For what seemed an eternity, Derek stood frozen with Tito's hand still clutching his arm.

Finally, Tito dropped his hand. "It's safe now. They rarely turn back."

"That happens often?"

"Most days they pass through," Tito said.

"I've never seen anything like that. What were they? Gorillas? Baboons?"

"A Bonobo family. Welcome to Africa," Tito answered as he began to run.

Derek fell into step with him, but his attention stayed on the spot in the bushes where the Bonobo monkeys had entered. In case Tito was wrong and the animals decided to come after them, he wanted a few seconds head start.

Not that he had any illusions that he could outrun a wild monkey, but he'd sure give it a shot if he had to.

"Will we encounter any other wild beasts?"

Tito shrugged. "Hard to say. Most are in the reserves but occasionally a cat will escape. Have to watch for snakes or rodents."

"Poisonous snakes?" He glanced at the dry grasses and moved farther to the center of the trail.

"Some. They rarely bother humans unless you trample through their territory."

"Don't the snakes eat the rats?"

"Our rats are big and huge with inch-long teeth," Tito said, demonstrating with his hands.

Derek saw the glint of mirth in Tito's dark eyes. "Yeah, right."

Tito laughed. "The rats carry disease and fleas. But the most dangerous creatures are the poachers."

"Poachers?"

Tito shrugged. "Big money in animal parts. The nearest reserve is miles away, so you need not worry."

"Great."

Wouldn't you know it? Gwen was right when she'd said it was dangerous out here. He was glad she'd insisted on sending Tito with him, though he wouldn't tell her that. Better to keep an adversarial barrier in their relationship.

He could imagine the expression on her face if he told her about the Bonobos. Probably wisest to keep that tidbit of adventure to himself, as well. He didn't want to give her any leverage over him.

Chapter Five

"Dr. Harper, this is Gwen." She adjusted Craig's cell phone to her ear, searching for better reception. She started walking away from the clinic.

"Gwen, is everything all right?" Dr. Harper's usually calm voice wavered slightly with concern.

"Yes. Fine," she answered, feeling the need to reassure him, not wanting to give him any reason to regret putting her in charge. She sat down on the stone bench near the kitchen where the reception came in clearer. "We're setting up. We'll open the doors soon. We had people lined up before the sun even rose this morning."

"Good. I wish I could be there with you."

Gwen heard the longing in his tone. Dr. Harper had dedicated so much to this organization. "Your leg will be healed in plenty of time for the next trip."

"True enough. This has actually been a blessing for Sally and I. It's forced us both to slow down and enjoy being together. We've even decided to take a cruise as soon as I'm up and about again."

Gwen smiled into the phone, happy for them but also because the potential for more responsibility loomed ever nearer. Though she couldn't stop the twinge of envy that shot through her at the thought of having someone to share her life with as she grew older. That dream had been shattered along with her innocence years ago. Pushing her dark musings aside, she kept her tone light. "That's wonderful, Dr. Harper. You and Sally haven't had a vacation in years."

"No, we haven't. How's Derek faring?"

"Well, I want to talk about Derek."

While she'd like to fill him in on how irritating and confusing she found his son, she kept her tone even. "Why didn't you tell me that he was here to run a race?"

There was a moment of silence before Dr. Harper sighed. "I should have at the airport, but there wasn't time. The race was the carrot I dangled to get Derek to agree to go on this trip."

"You mean he'd said no to the trip until you brought up the race?" Okay, any good thought she'd had about Derek just fizzled out. How could he be any more self-absorbed?

"No, no. I didn't think he'd agree unless he had another reason for going. I really want him to see the value of what we do."

Self absorbed *and* unmotivated to be here except for his own agenda. Great. The burden of her promise brought tension to her shoulders. "I need the details of the race. When, where and how he plans to get there."

"You'll have to ask him about that."

She dropped her head back and took a deep breath. Slowly exhaling, she tried to release her mounting frustration. She hated being unprepared. "I'll ask Derek when he gets back."

"Back?"

"He went for a run."

"Alone? You let him go off in the bush alone?" His voice rose with anxiety.

"Of course not," she said between her clenched teeth. His reaction was a natural fatherly one, but it still stung to hear the censure in his voice.

"Good, good. I knew I could count on you."

She rolled her eyes at the relief in his tone. Babysitting his son was not in her job description. This promise she'd made to her boss was proving more difficult to keep with each passing day.

"I'll check in with you in a couple of days," she said before hanging up and going back to work.

She walked down the line of people crowding the front door of the clinic, looking to make sure there were no life-threatening cases that should be seen immediately.

She'd situated a young villager named Mary at a table taking stats on those waiting to be seen. Then a patient would be directed to Gwen for diagnosis before being sent to see one of the doctors.

As much as she longed to be the one giving the care, Dr. Harper had made it clear from the beginning that her job was very important.

And having Moses and Ethan, who worked to keep the medical supplies fully stocked, was crucial, as well. Gwen took her place and gave Mary the go-ahead to start sending in patients.

Time slipped by and the heat rose in the cement-block clinic. Gwen wiped her forehead with the back of her hand. She gazed around at the work and realized how much personal gratification she gained from helping others.

In this small part of the world she was making a difference and being given the opportunity to tell others about Jesus and His saving grace just as Claire had done for her when she'd needed it the most.

A young mother carrying an infant in a sling tied at her slim shoulders sat down beside Gwen.

"When was the last time you took water?" Gwen had asked the question more than a dozen times in the last hour.

The woman—she had said her name was Tamara—thought for a moment. "Four days."

Gwen's insides clenched. She pinched some of the skin on the woman's arm with her thumb and index finger. The skin felt papery and stayed squeezed together after Gwen released her hold.

Dehydration.

Just like many of the others. Most of the villagers had been without water for days now. It didn't make sense. There was a well outside of town and a river coming off Lake Victoria that ran all the way to Rwanda not far away.

She directed the woman over to Craig, who would give her a shot of vitamin B and a bottle of water. She was thankful they'd arranged to have the bottled water, only they'd soon run out and have to drive to Kampala for more. But even that was a temporary solution.

She'd have to ask Moses and Ethan about the lack of water as soon as she could. Unfortunately, without Dr. Harper or even his son, they were shorthanded. She really needed Derek's help.

Where was he?

Gwen glanced at her watch. Forty minutes. Ha! They'd been gone over an hour now.

Her heart sped up and she forced herself to calm down. She tried not to think about the reasons that could keep the two runners from returning, but the image of some wild animal or some gun-toting rebel kept creeping into her mind. If they weren't back by noon, then she'd panic.

She focused on the people filling the clinic. Besides the villagers with dehydration, there were plenty of other illnesses to keep everyone hopping. She sent an elderly man with an infected cut over to Ned and a child with flulike symptoms to Joyce.

She counted at least three feverish patients she suspected had malaria and sent them over to Craig for medicine.

Frustration battered a steady beat in her head. The AIDS epidemic in Africa received so much coverage while malaria was rarely given any notice. The most disheartening part lay in the fact that the malaria disease was becoming resistant to traditional medicines.

Movement near the clinic doorway drew her attention. Derek stepped in, looking refreshed in long cargo shorts and a clean T-shirt, his hair still damp from a recent shower and his face cleanly shaven.

"It's about time," Gwen practically shouted as she stood. Heads turned and people stared, but she didn't care.

Derek raised a brow. "Miss me, did you?"

Gritting her teeth, she marched toward him and growled, "Hardly."

She would not tell him how distracted she'd been all morning waiting for him to return, worrying that he'd be eaten by a lion or kidnapped by some militant forces.

She never should have allowed him to go off, even with Tito along. She motioned for Moses to replace her at the table.

Pulling Derek by the arm, she led him back outside. "We need to talk."

He flashed a grin. "That sounds ominous."

Once they were far enough away from the clinic that they wouldn't be overheard, she stopped and planted her hand on her hips. "You're here for a race."

"Ah." He raised his chin slightly and his eyes took on a knowing gleam. "That's what has you all wound up."

"Why didn't you mention that you were only coming to run?"

"I tried to tell you earlier."

"And how long has this trip been planned?" She hated feeling as if she'd been misled, or at the very least, left out of the loop. Not being prepared made her nerves twitchy.

"Why should you know about that?" he said with a dismissive shrug as if she didn't matter.

His words assaulted her with the sting of

a slap to the face. She was responsible for his safety. For the success of the mission. For keeping a promise to his father that she wished she'd never made.

But what really sent her pulse shooting up was the taunting voice inside the dark memories of her soul, *You could die and nobody'd care.*

A flush of anger curled her hand into a fist. She struck out, her fist connecting with Derek's upper arm hard enough to make her knuckles scream with pain.

"Owww!" He covered the spot indignantly.

Instantly, mortification and shame rushed through her consciousness. She'd reacted in an old way. A way she'd tried so hard to control. She hadn't been prepared for his words to hurt or to stir up the past.

She watched the surprise and then the flash of anger light Derek's eyes. She stood her ground, accepting the consequences of her action, fully expecting him to retaliate.

He rubbed at his shoulder. "What was that for?"

She waited a heartbeat. Cataloging her confusion as to why he didn't hit her back, she charged ahead. "We are shorthanded without your father. And I'd at least expected you to want to learn what we were doing here even if you aren't medically trained. You're just deadweight to us now."

A shadow of annoyance crossed his face as he took a step forward. She lifted her chin. She would not back down.

"You are overreacting. I am here to learn. And I will. But I'm also here to win a race." He leaned closer, his eyes glittering. "Deal with it."

Breathing in sharply the minty tang of his breath, she stared into his face, noting the strong line of his smooth shaven jaw, his straight aristocratic nose and the little lines bracketing his clear green eyes. Her heart thumped in her chest, but there was no fear.

Something else, something foreign pulsed through her, something that scared her more than the thought of a physical blow.

Redirecting her thoughts, she asked,

"When and where is the race? And how do you plan to get there?"

He straightened, his jaw clenched. "I don't need you to micromanage me."

She raised a brow, realizing she'd struck a nerve. Interesting. "I need to know what to expect. Like it or not, I'm the leader of this trip."

His mouth curved at the corners in such a way that her heart did a little hiccup in her chest.

"I'll make sure you have all the pertinent details," he said. "Now, how can I help today?"

Wary of his charm, she contemplated her next move. She checked her watch. Almost noon. "Come on. Let's go."

Walking toward the kitchens with Derek striding along beside her, Gwen tried to come to terms with the fact that she'd punched Derek. She hadn't done anything like that in years. Regret for her childish behavior settled heavy on her shoulders.

"Derek, I'm sorry about before. For hitting you."

She wasn't sure what reaction she expected from her apology, but his silence made her feel small. The weight of his stare pressed down on her.

"Thank you for apologizing," he finally said. "I just want to know one thing."

"Okay. What?"

"How did you learn to pack such a wallop?" He flashed a grin. "You sure do have a mean right hook."

There were some stories best left untold. She shrugged. "Survival of the fittest and all that."

"Right. Like you ever had to fight to survive."

She slanted him a sharp glance. For a split second she thought about dispelling whatever assumptions he'd made about her life. Because she seemed well-adjusted and stable didn't mean her childhood had been.

But Derek wouldn't understand. How could he? He had loving parents and had grown up living the American dream. He'd never had to struggle for anything.

Nor had he ever felt the deep, lonely pain of having no one who loved you.

Telling him would serve no purpose.

Besides, she had no intention of having her past bandied about or worse yet getting back to his father. She didn't want to take the chance that Derek or his dad would judge her for her past.

Only one person knew the full truth of her life. Her friend and older sister, by choice if not by blood, Claire. Claire had understood, had experienced some of the same horrors and had helped Gwen to come to terms with that part of her life as a runaway.

So she kept her thoughts to herself. She waved at several children and accepted their hugs, giving the love she had in her to these little souls. She loved the children the most. She watched with interest the way Derek crouched to look one boy in the eye as the child showed him a car he'd made from recycled aluminum and other materials that were probably collected from garbage piles.

Derek's encouraging words to the boy won

him points with Gwen. Maybe he wasn't as totally self-absorbed as she thought.

They arrived at the kitchen building. Smoke continued to seep through the cracks in the brick and the spicy scent of curry wafted past. Gwen's stomach rumbled.

"Hmm. That smells tasty," Derek said as he peeked inside the open doorway.

Gwen walked inside. Several women were busy preparing the afternoon meal. Gwen waved at the woman cooking over the huge pot hanging above the open flames.

"Miss Gwen, it's so good to see you," one woman said as she came to hug Gwen. She wore a beautiful long tie-dyed shift with fringe around the neckline, while the hemline was adorned with an array of colorful beads. She wore her dark hair pulled back into a tight twist and her smooth brown skin glowed in the firelight.

"Hello, Mya. It's wonderful to see you, too." Keeping an arm around Mya's shoulder, Gwen said, "Mya, this is Derek Harper, Dr. Harper's son."

"Welcome." Mya reached out and took

Derek's hand. "We are sad your father was unable to come."

Derek smiled warmly. "I know he was sad he couldn't come, too."

"This is Mya," Gwen said. "She is part of Family in Crisis. Mya graduated from the university and comes to help us every year. We'd be lost without her dedication and wonderful cooking."

Mya laughed, a deep throaty sound. "You are too kind, Miss Gwen."

"I was hoping you'd take Derek under your wing for a bit."

Mya's brown eyes widened with surprise.

"Derek is here to learn all the different aspects of the clinic's mission and duties. I think starting here would be beneficial for him," Gwen explained to Mya. Then she turned her gaze to Derek, prepared to see anger or disbelief in his expression. Surely even he would guess that his seeing the kitchen wasn't a necessity right away. She could have waited and had him help when Ned or Craig came to help out.

Instead, amusement danced in his green

gaze. She blinked as confusion scattered her train of thought. "Uh, Derek…"

One side of his mouth quirked upward. "Yes?"

Giving herself a mental shake, she said, "Each team member takes a turn helping in the kitchen. We feed not only ourselves but the whole village when we are here."

"Sounds like a plan," he said. "So Mya, how can I help?"

Gwen stepped back as Mya began to explain the process of feeding an entire village of people. Gwen watched the intense way Derek listened and asked questions.

Pleasure swelled in her chest. He really was interested in what they were doing.

That was good. Really good.

Showing him the importance of the work would be that much easier.

And keeping a professional attitude toward him that much harder.

Even at dusk the air was warm as the sun set low in the sky, filling the world with incredible hues of red, orange and gold.

Derek sought the protection of a yellow-barked tree with palmlike branches that dappled the ground with fingered slivers of shade. He opened his PDA to type in his thoughts and observations.

Part of his father's expectation was that upon returning, Derek would submit a report on the mission.

Using the small keypad he noted his initial reaction to the clinic and to the villagers, citing the warmth with which the team had been welcomed, the organized way the team worked and how easily the members of Families in Crisis assimilated with the team.

He was impressed by the smooth way the women of the village, along with Family in Crisis, managed the kitchen and the feeding of the villagers, and the handling of the clinic by the Hands of Healing team.

From Derek's limited perspective, it was obvious all involved were committed to the work and to each other.

Especially Gwen.

She worked with tireless energy and always had a smile for those around her. It was amazing to watch the way she would comfort, encourage and support both those who crossed her path in the clinic but also those she encountered outside the clinic.

Everyone, that is, but him.

For some reason, ever since London… okay, before really, she'd been wary, suspicious and standoffish. But in London she seemed to have softened a bit. Not that he wanted her to be all cuddly. He found having a female not gushing over him or looking at him as though he was a tasty dessert—the way Joyce did—refreshing.

He'd already decided he wasn't looking to hook up with Gwen. So why did her reversion to her earlier attitude toward him now rub the wrong way?

"Hey, Harper!"

Derek looked toward the clinic doorway where Ned had stepped out. "Yeah?"

"Gwen." He pointed inside. "Come help." He disappeared back inside.

Derek shook his head. The man really needed to take a class or something to learn to communicate better. But he did get the gist of the message across. Time to join the team.

Derek saved his notes and headed toward the clinic building just as Tito came walking from the village. He was dressed for a run. Derek immediately stopped moving as his blood surged with the need to move.

"You coming or going?" he asked Tito.

Tito grinned. "Going. You wish to join to me?"

"Oh, yeah," Derek said. "Give me five minutes?"

At Tito's nod, Derek hustled to the clinic. A strong astringent scent filled the air. He paused as he watched the cleaning process. Moses mopped the floor. Craig wiped down the tables. Joyce and Mya were tidying the baskets holding the supplies. Gwen stood on a chair and wiped at the lights overhead.

"About time," she said without glancing toward him. "We're almost done already."

He gritted his teeth. "Good. Then you won't have a problem with me going for a run."

She pivoted, her gaze sharp, the motion causing the chair to wobble. She teetered for a second, her eyes went wide and her hands flailed, hitting the bare bulb and sending it swinging as the chair tipped.

Derek vaulted forward and caught her around the waist. She felt so fragile and vulnerable in his grip. Her hands landed on his shoulders, burning their imprint into his skin, and her amber gaze locked with his. He found himself fascinated with the gold-and-brown specks in her eyes.

A myraid of emotions flashed in her gaze; confusion, pleasure, wariness. And then, of all things, panic.

She shuddered and pushed against him. He set her down and she stepped back, putting distance between them.

"Thanks," she murmured, dropping her

gaze away from him. "Is Tito going with you?"

Confused by her sudden shift in attitude, he ran a hand through his hair. "Yes. He's outside waiting."

"Fine. Go. We're done here."

Aware of the others watching them, he nodded and headed to his room to change clothes. Minutes later he and Tito were hitting the trail hard. His body settled into a steady rhythm which freed up his mind to think.

He replayed those few moments in the clinic. One second Gwen was ready to act the offended taskmaster, and then she was sending him on his way.

He didn't understand her. And he assured himself he didn't want to…but that flash of panic wouldn't leave him. What was that about? Had she thought he'd hurt her? Had someone hurt her in the past?

Every latent protective instinct stirred, throwing off his stride. He forced himself back on pace and under control. He'd never done the hero thing and he certainly wasn't about to start now.

He refocused on the run and pushed Gwen from his thoughts.

Too bad it didn't work.

Chapter Six

Gwen sat on a rough log in front of the fire pit behind the clinic and relished the warmth on her feet. The strange dichotomy of Africa was that the days were scorching hot and the nights cool enough to warrant a sweater.

Every time she came here, she fell a bit more in love with the country and its people. How could a place so economically depressed be so full of life? The people had a joyful spirit even though their lives had none of the luxuries of the modern world. Maybe that was it. Maybe the simplicity of their world freed them to show love and joy.

The others had also gathered around the pit. Everyone except Derek.

He'd returned from his run and briefly stopped by before heading off to visit with Tito's cousin. She wasn't sure if he'd returned yet.

Joyce and Craig sat on a blanket with their backs propped by another gnarled log. Moses, Ethan and Ned sat in folding chairs brought out from the clinic.

To Gwen the most peaceful time of the day was when the team would sit and review the day's events, reassuring her she was doing a good job. The general consensus was that the first day was a success. They'd treated over a hundred and fifty people, fed closer to one-sixty and were looking forward to helping more.

Word would spread that the clinic was open and people from neighboring villages would start arriving. Many would walk a full day or more just for the opportunity to see the doctors.

Knowing now would be a good time to wash up since most everyone was outside which would give her a bit of privacy, she said good-night and headed to the bath-house, a stone-and-cement squat building that had plank floors so the water could drain into the hard ground beneath. They'd shipped jugs of water for bathing, which Derek had already used a good portion of, she noted with a twinge of worry.

She and the others were used to sponge bathing; she doubted Derek would like the idea. She'd have to fill him in on the rigors of mission life and the need to conserve their bathwater.

After a quick sponge off, she made her way through the darkened clinic, following the luminescence of the moon spilling out the open doors of the rooms lining the hall.

She slowed as she went by the room the guys stayed in and peered in, thinking perhaps Derek was inside. The room was empty. His little corner of the room was organized chaos. The covers on his bunk hastily thrown up to appear as if made. His clothes in tumbling piles on the floor. Shoes peeked out from under the cot.

Part of her was glad not to see him and part of her wanted to. When he was around she was full of conflicting impressions about him. At times he seemed pampered, almost spoiled, yet in London she'd glimpsed a more solid and grounded person.

Yes, he appeared reckless and rash but so disciplined with his education and training. He definitely had a physical prowess that even she found alluring.

Her cheeks burned at the memory of his hands spanning her waist when he'd kept her from falling off the chair earlier that day.

She'd felt secure in his grip, cared for.

She'd been mystified and pleased by the flash of interest in his gaze. Which had quickly turned to a deep probing stare that clarified the emerald in his eyes and made her feel as if he could see past the protective barricades she'd erected long ago to the defenseless girl inside.

A girl who had longed to be loved, to be cherished. A girl once full of trust and hope.

A girl who had nearly died one stormy night.

With a shudder, she hurried to her own room and readied herself for bed. She slipped between the cotton sheets on her foam mattress and tried to analyze what about Derek she found so unsettling. He'd never done anything to suggest he'd physically hurt her. He certainly could be a gentleman at times but also seemed to enjoy baiting her.

She didn't like the inconsistency of emotions he evoked in her. At times she felt comfortable with him and at other times he was a threat more real than the one in her nightmares.

She silently asked God to help her understand and know how to deal with Derek and the way she reacted to him.

Deliberately she turned her mind away from her strange responses to Derek and thought about the promise she'd made to his father. She hoped Derek would see how deeply their presence affected the people in Moswani.

Tomorrow she would have him work inside the clinic. She could only pray she'd be able to stay focused and not let his nearness disrupt the flow of the work.

After an especially invigorating morning run with Tito, Derek needed a shower, or at least a good dose of water dumped over his head. He noticed that Tito rubbed off the dirt and sweat with a towel rather than using water. Interesting place, this Africa.

Entering the stone-walled bathhouse, Derek expected to see the jugs of water the team had brought in that he'd been using for washing. But instead he found a bucket half full of water and a metal cup.

A square sheet of paper lay on a table beside the bucket. He picked up the note and as he read the tight, neat script, his eyebrows rose.

It seemed Gwen was putting him on water restriction. She couldn't control his runs so now she wanted to control his showers? He tightened his fist and crumpled the note with a good dose of irritation.

Shoving the wad of paper in the pocket of his running shorts, he contemplated the best use of the water and his towel. Well, if it was good enough for Tito to just rub off the dirt, then it was for him, as well.

Derek decided to save the water for after his evening run in the hopes he'd have a full bucket of water to really scrub with.

When he was done and dressed in light-weight cargo shorts and a white T-shirt, he went to find Gwen to see what she had planned for him today. She seemed to thrive on being in control. Well, he'd let her have her way unless she interfered with his plans.

A line twice as long as the one the day before had formed at the clinic door. As he passed through he noted the varying ages and manner of dress of the Ugandans. Some men and women were dressed in what would be considered normal for America—cotton pants or jeans and printed button-down shirts for the men and simple cotton dresses for the women—many more people wore brightly colored, patterned outfits that fit in with his image of African culture.

And yet some used tattered remnants

of cloth to cover themselves. Clearly there was an economic imbalance among the populace.

Pondering the diversity of the Africans, he squeezed into the clinic past a table where the woman whom Gwen had introduced to him as Mary sat filling out the statistic forms on each patient.

He glanced at the stack of forms already completed and noted with gratitude they were written legibly, which would serve him well once they returned to the States and he sat down to write out a report based on the information provided.

Derek found Gwen sitting at another table, talking with an elderly woman. The woman's graying hair was held back beneath a shocking pink scarf and her long dress of a vivid blue made Derek think briefly of a beautiful bird. Gwen held the older lady's hand and compassion softened the edges of Gwen's mouth and brightened the amber of her eyes.

She glanced up and saw him. The small smile she sent him worked to send his pulse pounding as effectively as the blast of a starter gun. Odd that something as insignificant as a casual smile from the redhead could cause such a reaction in him.

Gwen waved him over. He approached as the elderly woman stood then wobbled. He rushed forward to steady her.

"Thank you, young man," she said in slightly accented English.

"You're welcome," he replied with a smile.

"Would you help Thelma over to Ned?" Gwen asked as she handed him a paper.

"Of course," Derek replied. Taking the paper, he offered his arm to Thelma and noticed the woman's ankles were puffy and discolored. They shuffled their way the short distance to where Ned sat stitching up a gash on a young girl's leg.

As Derek waited with Thelma leaning on his arm, he glanced at the paper that listed Thelma's symptoms and Gwen's diagnosis of diabetes, plus dehydration.

Once he'd transitioned Thelma to Ned's

care, Derek returned to Gwen. She now spoke with a man whose arm hung at an odd angle. From the conversation, Derek gathered that the man's arm had broken some time ago and needed to be rebroken to heal properly.

Derek's gut rolled a bit at the thought, but he gamely led the man to wait for Craig. Derek gave the paper Gwen had given him to Moses, who was helping Craig. Moses frowned as he read the notes, but spoke kindly and with confidence to the man, reassuring him they would do their best to make it so he could once again use his arm.

For the rest of the day, Derek remained in the role of guide, showing each patient to where Gwen indicated. Several times he wondered why she wasn't treating patients; surely she wanted to use her medical training to help those in need.

Later that night as they gathered after the meal around the fire, Derek commented that many of those they'd seen that day were given water and a vitamin B shot.

Moses explained about the river drying out. "One day the water flows strong then slowly it died away." His voice held a note of resignation.

"How long has the river been dry?" Joyce inquired. She was dressed in jeans and a long-sleeved shirt and sat on a metal folding chair.

Moses shrugged his big shoulders. He sat on a blanket with his long legs stretched out before him and his hands braced behind him in a reclined position. "Long time."

"How have the villages been getting water up to this point?" Craig asked as he fiddled with his CD player after taking a seat next to Moses.

Moses and Ethan exchanged glances. Ethan shifted on the log before speaking. "Once a week someone travels to the border and barters for barrels of water. That water is then rationed among the villagers."

Remorse for the way he blithely used

water as he would at home hit Derek in the gut like a sucker punch.

"And every village does this," Derek stated quietly, knowing that it was true.

He tried to wrap his mind around the unmet need of something so basic as water. No wonder Gwen had cut his bathwater to a half bucket. He glanced at her across the flames of the fire. She met his gaze with understanding in her amber-colored eyes. The glowing light glittered in her long red braid.

She'd known all along how limited the water supply was, and yet had not ordered him to stop using so much. Instead she had discreetly gotten her point across. Appreciation tightened in his chest.

"What about the well?" Gwen asked, her amber gaze sparked with concern as she turned her attention to Ethan.

"Boarded up. Without the river, the well is useless."

She bit her lip for a moment before turning to Craig. "How much water do we have?"

"At the rate we're giving it out, I'd say five more days' worth."

"Moses, can you contact your people in Kampala and have them send us more bottled water?"

"Yes. In the morning I will send word."

Derek saw an opportunity and seized it. "I need to go into Kampala on Saturday. I could bring some back. Wouldn't that be faster?"

Gwen gave him a hard stare. "We're all needed here."

He arched a brow. "I'm not. I need to go anyway."

She scoffed. "I can't let you go alone."

He gritted his teeth. "I'm sure Tito needs to go, as well."

Moses spoke up. "Yes, Tito and his cousin could go with you. That would be a good solution."

"I agree," Ethan said. "Though, Dr. Harper's son, we do need you. You work hard and the people like you."

Surprised by the compliment, Derek blinked. "Thank you. And please, call me Derek."

Ethan grinned, showing big white even teeth. "Derek, then."

"I still don't think—" Gwen started to protest.

Annoyed that once again she wanted to control the situation and him, Derek cut her off. "That's the problem, Gwen. You think too much."

Her eyes narrowed. "I don't take my responsibilities lightly."

"Would you like to take this outside the circle, Ms. Yates?" He stood.

Swiftly she rose and walked a few feet away, leaving him to follow her. He went on the offensive.

"Are you suggesting I take responsibility lightly?" From her tone he knew that was exactly what she was suggesting.

"I don't think you take Hands of Healing very seriously."

He narrowed his own gaze. "I've lived with the presence of Hands of Healing hanging over my head for more than sixteen years. Believe me, I take it seriously enough."

"Hanging over your head? What is that supposed to mean?"

Realizing he'd let slip some of the bitterness he felt for his father's "other child," he shook his head. "Nothing."

"It's obviously something." Her head cocked to the side, she regarded him with undisguised interest. "Why did you come on board with Hands of Healing if you find it such a burden?"

Aware of the audience witnessing and no doubt hearing their bickering, he took a deep breath and slowly let it out. "What I find a burden, Gwen, is your need to micromanage everyone."

Outrage heightened the color in her cheeks to a rose hue. "I don't micromanage." She turned her gaze on the others sitting around the fire and yelled, "Do I micromanage?"

"Well…" Joyce winced. "Maybe a bit."

"But in a good way," Craig was quick to add.

Ned threw him a disapproving look before saying, "Leadership is hard."

Moses chuckled and addressed Gwen. "*You* remind me of Dr. Harper."

Derek should have felt smug that the others had confirmed his pronouncement. But as he saw Gwen's crestfallen expression his insides twisted and he found himself wanting to take back his words.

"You do remind me of Dad in some ways. You're intense like he is. I see why he has such trust in you," he said, hoping to make up for his earlier barb.

She gave him a tight smile. "So I suppose while you're in Kampala you'll find out more about your race?"

"Race?" Joyce leaned forward. "When, where? Give us details."

"Yes," he said to Gwen. They stared at each other for a moment, her gaze unreadable. Finally, she turned away and marched back to her place by the fire.

As he reclaimed his own spot, he addressed Joyce's question. "I don't have all the details yet."

Moses inquired about the competition and the conversation turned to running and other sports. Derek was aware when Gwen murmured a good-night and slipped quietly away from the group. He watched her lithe form disappear inside the clinic.

Why did you come on board with Hands of Healing if you find it such a burden?

Her question reverberated through his mind. Purposely, determinedly, he pushed the words away. The answer was too complicated and too painful to even consider.

"Hey, where are all the people?" Derek asked as he and Tito returned from their morning run. For the last few mornings when they reentered the village there had been a growing line of people waiting to be seen. But not today.

"Today's Sunday. Everyone's at the church," Tito replied. "Come on, we should hurry. Service will start soon."

Not sure going into a church while hot and sweaty was appropriate, Derek couldn't deny he was curious. So he followed Tito to the other side of the village.

A square, brick building with glassless windows stood off to one side. Derek could see that the interior was bursting with people. He and Tito squeezed in at the back.

It wasn't hard to notice the Hands of Healing team scattered in various sections of the sanctuary. His gaze focused on Gwen. She sat near the front, her red hair unmistakable. She had on the same flowery outfit she'd worn in London. He remembered that night with fondness.

Since there were no places left to sit on the wooden benches, Derek and Tito leaned against the back wall along with several others. Derek was glad he didn't have to worry about his shoes tracking in dust since the floor was hard-packed dirt.

A couple of men and women moved to the front of the church. The men began a rhythmic beat on beautifully carved drums and the women played various other instruments—some type of harp, a wind instrument that looked like a hybrid of a flute and a clarinet. People began to sing.

The melodic raised voices filled the

church and spilled out through the open windows. Derek closed his eyes and listened, enjoying the music. The singing went on for a long time until a man moved to the front. He laid his Bible on the podium and then began to preach.

Derek listened with interest. The pastor didn't use outlines or PowerPoint overheads as was the fashion in most churches in the States that Derek had attended. This man spoke from his heart, talking about God's call on their lives.

"The Lord speaks but you do not listen. Like Samuel, you do not recognize the Lord. Wake up! You must be alert!"

On he went, his passionate sermon stirring the congregation. Derek tried to understand, but he'd never heard the Lord and was sure God had never spoken directly to him.

When the pastor finished, the singing resumed. Joyful songs full of praise that uplifted Derek's spirit. He felt rejuvenated and ready to dive in to help.

As the service broke up, Derek waited

for Gwen and the others to file past. Gwen's eyes widened and then she smiled. "I'm so glad you made it back in time," she said as they walked back toward the clinic.

"Me, too. That was incredible."

Her pleased expression warmed him. He excused himself to clean up and returned a short while later. He found the work in the clinic to be interesting and rewarding.

For the next few days Derek settled into a routine. After his runs, he'd work in the clinic helping where needed and making notes of ways to improve the flow of traffic within the clinic.

He and Gwen seemed to circle each other like caged animals. She, the tigress and he, well, he couldn't decide what animal he'd want to be likened to, but the tension between them sparked conflicting emotions in him that made his runs that much more productive.

As if he could run into the ground the growing admiration he had for her and trample over the annoyance he felt every time she bossed him around because he knew he was coming up short in her eyes.

Okay, to be fair she didn't boss, she asked.

Yet her tight-reined approach to management still grated. And it wasn't that she was female. He knew that with certainty. There was something, though. Something that rose up to bug him and he couldn't get a bead on it.

They'd all finally agreed that Tito and his cousin Al would drive Derek into Kampala where they'd purchase more water and Derek and Tito could register for the upcoming marathon.

Gwen had reluctantly given her approval but, only after Ned had stated that Derek going was a good idea. Apparently she valued his opinion. Derek refused to admit that he wanted her to value *his* opinion, as well.

But in Gwen's typical controlling fashion, she'd declared they could wait a few more days.

At night as they would gather around

the fire pit, he'd stare at Gwen and try to understand her. But then she'd return his stare and he'd find himself fascinated with the gold specks in her eyes, the way her mouth formed a smile and the dancing firelight in her hair. And whatever gnawed at him would dissipate with the fire's smoke.

Tito had started joining them at night, along with several other Africans. The discussions were interesting and lively.

One night a young, brash boy who'd joined them asked, "Where is your cowboy hat?"

"Excuse me?" Derek stared at the kid.

"You Americans wear cowboy hats and drive big cars, right?"

"Where did you get that idea?" Derek asked, wondering if a Texan missionary had come through at one time.

"My cousin lives in the city. There is television there. We watch the American shows. The one about the Carrington family. The big cars, the big houses, the big hats. Do all Americans live like that?"

Derek restrained himself to a chuckle so as not to offend the boy. "No. That is a made up show called *Dynasty*. Americans are not like that. Most people live in modest houses and very few people wear big hats."

That prompted a discussion on the views the Africans had of America. Derek came to realize the impressions most had were from the few televisions available and from missionaries or medical personnel like themselves. He understood how the different portrayals of America left many confused.

One night as they gathered around the fire, more people squeezing in, Derek found himself sitting beside Gwen. She had her shoulders turned away from him as she conversed with a woman holding a child. Gwen's voice was low and soothing. Her braid hung down her back, little curls escaping around the nape of her neck.

She wore no jewelry or cloying perfume. She was no-nonsense and organized, reserved and cautious. Kind and considerate. She had a tremendous work ethic and an impressive ability to keep others calm.

As he contemplated slipping the rubber band from her hair and seeing how the mass would look loose, he accepted that he'd been right the other night when he'd said Gwen was in many ways like his father.

And that probably was the crux of why she bugged Derek so much. She reminded him of his failure to be the person his father wanted him to be.

That realization knocked the breath from his lungs. He was sure Dr. Phil would have a field day with such a revelation.

Okay, so he'd been harboring some resentment toward his father's newest protégé. Now that he'd realized it he'd work to let it go. Resenting Gwen for the way his father admired and preened over her wasn't fair to her.

Tomorrow, he decided, he'd do something nice for her. And maybe it would be the start of a new friendship.

Or maybe not.

Chapter Seven

"What are you doing?" Gwen stared at Derek in dismay as she watched him drag the table she normally used over to butt up against the table that Mary used.

"Making some changes," Derek replied with a quick flash of a smile.

He still wore his running gear and his T-shirt showed signs of his exertion. Obviously, he and Tito must have just returned from their predawn run. She should have been repulsed by all that sweaty male-ness; instead, she found his musky scent mingled with the African earth invigorating.

Or perhaps it was the fact that her world seemed suddenly altered that made her feel slightly light-headed. She forced her mind from Derek and onto the situation. "Why?"

He moved past her and brought over a stack of folding chairs. "Because change is good."

"You're here to learn, not reorganize and change things."

He ignored her statement.

She stared as he unfolded chair after chair and arranged them on one side of the tables. Change was not good unless one prepared for it.

She grabbed his arm as he bent to unfold the last chair. "Stop. Tell me, what are you doing?"

He straightened, his expression patient, kind. A look she'd seen him give to others but not her.

Suspicion gathered at the edges of her mind. Why now? What did he want from her?

He gently pried her hand from his arm.

She was mortified to see the imprint of her fingers where they'd dug into his flesh. She opened her mouth to apologize, but he kept hold of her hand, the warm pressure flowing through her veins and scattering her thoughts.

"Let me explain. I've been observing the way you've been running the clinic, and though it's been working, I think I've come up with a better system."

She frowned, stung by the criticism. "Your father has always run the clinic this way."

He nodded. "I understand that. But my system will be better."

She shook free of his hold and stepped back. "You want to one-up your father?"

He gave her a confused glare. "No. I'm trying to utilize my skills here. Problem solving is what I do."

"We didn't have a problem for you to solve," she huffed.

"Just hear me out." He led her to the table where he grabbed a pencil and a blank piece of paper. He made a diagram of dots.

"See this circle," he said as he poised the pencil on it. "This is Mary. People come here first. She takes information one person at a time. Then the person moves to this dot." He drew a line connecting the dots. "This is you. Now you talk with that person."

"Right. I diagnose them and send them on to one of these dots," she said, pointing with her finger. "I get it. It works."

"But not as efficiently as it could."

He drew more dots next to the first set. Only this time the first dot was accompanied by four more dots. And then four more dots, spaced apart from each other, appeared.

"Now, you have five people taking information and sending the patients on to see the doctors," he said with a triumphant grin.

She frowned, feeling as though the earth beneath her feet had somehow turned to quicksand. "But who will determine who sees which doctor?"

He tapped the pencil in the air at her. "Good question. I found out that Mary has had some nursing training and she knows several other women with some medical background who are willing to help."

"But how will they know what to look for and which doctor to send people to? That's my job." Her mind scrambled, trying to see how she would fit in to this scheme of his. Ever since the first trip, Dr. Harper had assigned her the task of diagnosing and directing the patients.

He hitched a hip on the side of the table. "You and the other doctors would have to give a quick lesson, tell them what to look for, what questions to ask."

She felt displaced. This was happening too fast. "We can't do this right now. People are already lining up outside to be seen. We don't have time."

"We'll make time," he countered, his dark eyes probing at her. "This will be faster, more efficient. Hands of Healing will be able to serve a greater number of people. Isn't that the goal?"

She stared at his diagrams, admitting, that yes, the initial contact would run smoother.

She had to put her own needs aside for the good of the mission. "Yes. But…"

"What's really bothering you about this, Gwen?"

She shook her head and kept her gaze down, not sure how to put words to the crazy sense of unease squeezing her chest. She needed time to process through this.

He lifted her chin with the crook of a finger, his mouth curved in a soft melting smile. "I freed you up to do what you were meant to do, Gwen. Help people. See patients."

The fourth dot.

She would be the fourth doctor. That made sense. That would be great. More than great. She would be able to use her skills. Skills she'd honed back in Seattle at Dr. Harper's clinic.

"I was hoping you'd be pleased."

His softly spoken words tried to pry loose the tightness under her ribs. Again she stepped back, forcing his hand to fall away and the safety of distance to fill the gap between them. "Why would you want to please me?"

"Because I'm a nice guy."

"And full of yourself."

"Hey, no need to get nasty," he said with mock hurt lacing his words.

"Oh, like you weren't nasty the other night when you picked on me?"

"I did not pick on you."

"Did, too," she huffed. "I asked you a perfectly valid question which you dodged by picking on me."

"You're right, I did," he said, his expression rueful. "But it's only because you're so easy."

Her chin dropped. "Excuse me?"

"You take offense to everything I say."

She scoffed. "I do not."

One corner of his mouth curled. "*Almost* everything."

"That is so not true." Was it? She didn't want to think of herself as easily provoked. She wanted to be an approachable person. Someone others could trust. Like Claire. She earned Gwen's trust with patience, dedication and unconditional love.

Derek had said she was intense like his dad. Dr. Harper could be intimidating at times, but he was solid and trustworthy. She respected him for that.

Claire had told her often that she worked too hard and needed to relax more. But how could she relax when there was so much at stake?

During college, she'd devoted herself to her studies, which was reflected in her grades. In her profession as a Physician's Assistant she had to be thorough and on top of her game because a mistake could be deadly.

"Hey, now. I didn't mean to upset you," Derek said, his voice full of concern. "I was just teasing you."

She gave him a weak smile, realizing she'd been away from her family for too long. Nick, Claire's husband, and Tyler, both liked to tease her. At first she hadn't known how to deal with it but she'd realized after a while it was one way they showed their affection for her.

Surely Derek's teasing had nothing to do with affection. Maybe teasing was a male thing.

Derek stood and tugged on her braid. "Come on, Gwennie. Let's go round up the troops."

A lump formed in her throat as she watched him walk away.

No one but her parents had ever called her Gwennie.

The new clinic system was up and running and Derek felt a sense of satisfaction grow inside his chest. In his own way he was helping, making a difference. Derek found his place helping Moses and Ethan keep the supplies stocked and the patients calm.

At times he felt totally incompetent and in awe of the doctors as they dealt with the diseases and injuries flooding through the clinic. Derek had never been exposed to people with AIDS, malaria, tuberculosis or Ebola before. He was thankful for the protective gear the staff all wore, because whatever ailment the person had didn't change the amount of care or attention they were given. He really wished he could have seen his father in action.

Maybe on the next trip.

He was a little shocked to discover he wanted to be a part of the team again.

Strange.

At noon, the clinic closed for meals. Since the number of meals given out each day was growing, Derek had enlisted the aid of some of the younger women and men to help Mya and the other women in the kitchen. He was getting used to the limited diet of rice and dried beans, cornmeal and Matoke.

Ned had explained in his very precise way that eating the fresh vegetables the Africans grew would make the Americans sick because the soil contained toxins that the westerners wouldn't be able to tolerate.

Derek had no desire to compromise his digestive system, not with the race fast approaching. But he was thankful he'd thought to pack a box of protein bars in his bag.

At the end of every day, he'd help with the cleaning of the clinic and eat with the others. Then he and Tito would take off on their second run of the day. This routine went on for the next three days. He was relieved and content with the easy, fairly amiable relationship he and Gwen had forged.

Sometimes he swore she said things to provoke him, but he stayed in control and refrained from teasing her, even if he had to bite his tongue to keep from popping off with a remark that he would bet she'd take offense to. He liked the way her eyes flashed when she was indignant.

He tried to look for other ways he could be useful. One evening as he and Tito headed off in a new direction, he saw what he assumed was the well.

Derek slowed and jogged over to it. As Moses had stated, the top was boarded up.

"Hold up," Derek called to Tito. Derek tested the boards, they wouldn't budge. He found the places where the nails had been hammered in. There were slits between the two boards. He bent and picked up a small rock and wedged it through the opening until it dropped then bent close to listen.

Tito trotted over. "Something wrong?"

Derek held his finger to his lips. Faintly he heard a small splash. Not dried up. He straightened with a grin.

"Everything's good. Come on. I'll beat you back," he challenged and set off with one thought running through his mind: tomorrow he'd come back with something to pry open the apparently no longer useless well.

Dusk fell and so did the temperature. Gwen pulled on a hoodie and a pair of sweats before heading outside for the night downtime by the fire pit.

The number of people gathered before the fire had grown as many of those who had traveled to the clinic stayed, sleeping on pallets under the trees or on the floor of the clinic or cookhouse. It wasn't unusual for people to stay until the doctors left.

Many had made a long journey to be seen and relished the food and comfort provided by Hands of Healing. The importance of what they were doing empowered her determination to give the best care possible.

Gwen meandered through the people, giving words of encouragement and listening to their stories. She noted Derek's absence and figured he'd show up later as he had the last few nights after his run.

She couldn't fathom the dedication and discipline to push himself the way he did when he had to be as exhausted by the end of the day as the rest of them. His running obviously meant a great deal to him. She admired his steadfastness; it said a lot about the kind of man he was.

She owed him a thank-you and an apology for the system he'd insisted they implement in the clinic. The thank-you because it really worked well. They were seeing more people and she gained so much personal satisfaction from the hands-on care she was able to provide.

And the apology for being so resistant to change. She'd known so much chaos in her life that she hated not to be prepared for what was coming next. But apparently God was stretching her with Derek and his system.

She just wished she could get a pulse on Derek's inner thoughts. Did he really understand how much good they were doing? Did he see the people and value them, or was all of this just part of him doing his time until he could move on to his race and whatever else he had in mind?

Because she knew there was something.

His avoidance of her question about why he had come aboard Hands of Healing still rankled. But she'd had little opportunity to broach the subject again. He seemed to be making a point of keeping their interactions strictly superficial.

He'd stopped teasing her, even when she dropped comments that should have goaded a smart-aleck comeback.

She shouldn't be disappointed. She should be glad.

She didn't want their relationship to be any more than it was. Still…she missed the bantering.

Smoke from the fire curled in a ribbon upward toward the darkening sky. She sat down on a woolen blanket next to Mya. They chatted easily for a while. Then someone began to sing in English, Uganda's official language. Others joined in and someone produced a drum made from animal hide stretched over a hollow tree trunk.

Gwen lifted her voice to the familiar words of the old hymn, enjoying the praiseful worship. The song shifted as the locals began to sing in Lugandan, their native tongue. Gwen listened to the rhythmic beat of the drum and the lyrical voices.

Her gaze strayed to the bush. Where was Derek? He usually arrived by now.

Anxiety formed a tight knot in the pit of her stomach. Thoughts of all the bad things that could happen to him swamped her. He could get attacked by a wild animal or fall and break something. She didn't even want to think about him being taken by the rebels in Moswani or the Ugandan militia.

Thankfully, they'd been undisturbed by the civil war so far. But that didn't mean life couldn't turn on a dime. She forced down the sense of panic that thought created.

The clinic had a plan in case of an attack, though as far as she knew, they'd never had to implement it. She prayed they never would.

So where was Derek? Maybe he'd come back and turned in for the night already.

She rose and left the crowd behind as she walked toward the clinic, intending to check if Derek was inside or not. She froze as the moon's glow fell on the shadows of three people walking out of the bush.

It took a moment for her eyes and her brain to make out the tall gangly form of Tito, the stooped stature of an elderly man, and Derek carrying a young child in his arms.

She rushed forward. "What happened?"

"He needs your help, Gwennie," Derek said as he continued on with purposeful strides toward the clinic.

Gwen hurried to enter before him and turn on the overhead lights. She grabbed some gloves and a gown as Derek settled the boy on an exam table. She gave a small gasp as she took in the little one's mangled leg and extended abdomen.

"How did this happen?" she asked.

"A tree fell on him," supplied the old man.

His grizzled gray hair and watery brown eyes filled with anguish and caught at Gwen's heart. She began to examine the child. His breathing was shallow and labored, his pulse thready.

"How long ago?" She looked to the grandfather for the answer.

"I'm not sure," he replied. "I had left for a few days and when I came back he was gone. I went to look for him and found him. I got the tree off him and began the journey here. That was two days ago."

"We found them on the side of the trail," Derek supplied.

Her heart squeezed more. "This leg is pretty bad. I think he's bleeding internally. Tito, go get Moses and the other doctors," she called to the young runner hovering in the doorway. "Derek, find Mya and have her boil some water."

He nodded and disappeared behind Tito. She turned to the old man. "Where are his parents?"

He held her gaze. "Gone."

She read the true meaning of that word in his brown eyes. Gone meant dead. "Are you related to the boy?"

"My grandchild, Cam."

"Good." They would need to type the old man and if he matched the boy, they would use his blood for a transfusion if it came to that.

Within moments the clinic was busy with the team trying to save the child's life. Ned worked to stop the internal bleeding, Craig and Gwen worked on the leg, resetting the multiple fractures and stitching up the lacerations. Joyce typed the grandfather's blood and confirmed a match, then began a transfusion.

Gwen glanced up several times to see Derek standing watch in the corner, his eyes clouded with distress.

A few hours before dawn, the team had done all they could with the limited resources they had, and now they had to wait and pray. Everyone had slowly gone off to catch some sleep.

Gwen stayed. She stripped off the gown, gloves and mask she'd donned. Hours earlier she'd removed her hoodie in favor of the plain white tank top underneath. Her eyes felt gritty and her muscles tense. She rolled her shoulders and went back to the boy's side, checking his pulse, his breathing.

In a nearby chair the boy's grandfather, James, slept. She placed a blanket over him.

"You were awesome in there," Derek said as he came up behind her.

His praise washed over her, easing a bit of the tension. She turned with a smile and drank in the sight of him. He still wore his running clothes. His unshaven face couldn't hide the fatigue in his expression. He'd carried that child here, and she was certain he'd saved Cam's life.

During the long hours that they'd worked on the boy, Derek had been there, silently offering his support. Tenderness swelled under her breastbone. "Thanks."

"Will he live?"

"I pray so," she replied on a yawn.

"Here," he said, looping his arm around her shoulders and steering her toward the hall. "You're exhausted. You should rest. I'll stay up with him."

He was big, warm and comforting. For a single instant the temptation to snuggle against him enfolded her but just as quickly the invasion of her personal space sent waves of unease sliding over her skin.

She ducked under his arm and stepped away, rubbing at the prickles on her arms. "You don't have to do that. It's my job."

His expression hardened slightly. "Look, this isn't about who's in control. You're dead on your feet. What good will you be come sunrise if you don't get some sleep?"

She didn't have an answer to that. He was right, of course. She'd be no good to anyone tomorrow if she didn't rest. "Why don't you at least go clean up and then when you come back, I'll go?"

His mouth softened into a lazy smile. "I stink that bad, huh?"

"I didn't mean that," she said. "You don't smell. Not that I was checking. I mean, I just thought you'd want to change into something more comfortable."

"I was teasing you, Gwennie," he drawled quietly as he stepped closer and twined her braid around his hand. "You are my priority. You need sleep more than I need a shower."

Heat infused her cheeks and pleasure unfurled in her veins and she ignored the little voice that cautioned he was too close. Dangerously close. Physically and emotionally.

She should tell him to stop calling her Gwennie, but she was too tired and he was too near, so near she could see the pulse beating at the base of his tanned neck.

And he'd finally teased her again.

Time to make a hasty retreat before she did something foolish like stagger into his arms.

She stepped back but was brought up short by her braid still wrapped in his grasp. He stepped closer as he tugged her forward. Her breath snagged on the intake. He leaned toward her.

She watched his mouth and thought she should do something, should be afraid or at least feel crowded, but all she felt was a tingling of anticipation scatter through her whole being.

She dared not close her eyes. She wanted to be prepared for his kiss.

He gently touched his nose to hers, his green eyes reflecting a shimmering glow from the overhead fluorescents. He lifted his chin a fraction and lightly dropped a kiss on her forehead.

As he had the last time.

She opened her mouth to protest as disappointment spiraled through her like an out-of-control top. She wanted to tell him she was ready for him to kiss her. To tell him this was a big step for her. But he released her braid, planted his hands on her shoulders, spun her around and gave her a gentle push toward the hall.

"Try to sleep, Gwennie."

Yeah, right! She shuffled down the hall to her room, collapsed on the mattress and buried her burning face in the pillow.

Chapter Eight

Derek shifted again in the too-small, uncomfortable folding chair. A glance at his watch told him it was almost time to meet Tito for their morning run. Might as well bag trying to sleep. He rose and stretched his aching muscles.

Poor Grandpa James must have been beyond exhausted to find rest in the folding chair he slept in. The boy, Cam, lay on the examination table, a blanket drawn over him and his broken leg propped up. Derek moved to Cam's side and lightly placed a hand on the boy's forehead.

His skin was still warm but not burning

the way it had been when Derek had first touched him. Derek knew enough about medicine and the human body to know it wasn't good to sustain a high fever.

"Thank You, God, that we found him," Derek whispered. He closed his eyes and continued. "Please heal this boy, Lord."

He stood there for several moments with his eyes closed and his hand touching the child. He wasn't sure what he was waiting for, some sign that God heard him, maybe.

Finally, he left the clinic and went in search of something to pry open the well. Near the kitchen house he found a flat metal bar that had been tossed in the woodpile. Before going to meet Tito, he grabbed two empty water jugs and a ball of twine he'd found in the medical supplies.

He met up with Tito as the youth came trotting from his cousin's house.

He handed a jug to Tito. "We're going to bring back some water and see if it's usable."

They set off, their pace moderate but

slowly building speed as they went. Before long they reached the well. Using the metal bar, they pried the planks of wood from the top. Derek knotted one end of the twine around the handle of a jug and lowered the container.

He prayed that the bottom wouldn't be too far below. The jug bobbled. Derek jiggled the string, hoping some water would fill the jug. He reeled the jug up and grimaced at the mud caking the outside and the barest amount of liquid sloshing inside.

"This isn't going to work," he grumbled.

"Maybe you should try this?" Tito held up a wooden bucket attached to a long, thick rope.

"Funny." Derek grabbed the bucket from the grinning African teen.

With the bucket, he made short work of filling the jugs. He examined the murky water, never more grateful for the water filtration system back home.

"Yuck," he said. He hoped Gwen and the others had some method for purifying the water. He didn't think boiling would be enough.

"Let's go see what the doctors can do with this." Derek handed a full jug to Tito and they headed back toward the village.

The morning sun grew round in the sky, its golden rays touching the dewy drops of moisture on the blades of tall grass and oval-shaped leaves of the trees. A huge bird with an enormous wingspan landed off to Derek's left on the top of a gnarled palm tree.

Derek slowed to get a better look. The gray wings of the bird folded closed, his red breast puffed out and his squawk rent the air.

"You losing steam, old man," Tito called over his shoulder as he continued onward, his long legs moving in a rhythmic stride.

"Not a chance," Derek retorted and resumed his pace. Soon he caught up to Tito, grinned at the young man and then put on the steam and passed him by.

They slowed as they neared the village. More people gathered in a long line at the door of the clinic. The village itself stood off to the side, the many small stone-and-mud huts placed in haphazard array without any real designated main thoroughfare.

One structure with a thatched roof and clay walls had tables set up outside with pairs of shoes lined up. Moses had explained earlier in the week when Derek had commented on it that several years before some missionaries came through and taught the man how to make shoes. For the price of a chicken anyone could walk away with a new pair.

Smoke from the kitchen house puffed out from the gaps in the bricks and the now-familiar scent of mashed bananas wafted on the breeze. His stomach rumbled. Joyce stepped out and waved him over.

Taking the jug from Tito, he headed for the kitchen. "Good morning, Joyce," he called.

"Morning. You should go over to the clinic. The boy is awake," she said.

"Thanks, I will."

As he approached the clinic he set the jugs of water down near the back corner of the building. He'd check on the child and then show Gwen the water.

The child was indeed awake, his chocolate-brown eyes alert as Derek approached. Grandpa James shuffled forward and threw his arms around Derek in a bear hug. "Thank you. We are in your debt."

A little embarrassed by the gratitude, Derek patted the older man's stooped shoulders. "I'm glad we happened to run that route yesterday."

James stepped away and wiped at the tears in his eyes. "Doctor say Cam wouldn't have lived much longer if you hadn't found us."

"God's timing is perfect," Gwen said as she stepped into the room.

Her words struck a chord inside Derek's soul. It did seem too coincidental that they would take a new route at the exact time they were needed.

His father always touted that there were no coincidences, only God sequences. That everything in life happened for a reason even if we don't understand why or see the pattern.

Derek was grateful to think God had used him to save Cam's life.

What purpose did God have for bringing him and Gwen together?

"Have you eaten, James?" Derek asked.

"No. I must stay with my boy," he replied and went back to the chair.

"I'll bring you some food, if that's okay with Gwennie," Derek said as his gaze slid to his favorite doctorly type.

"Of course that would be okay," she said with a smile full of approval. "That's very kind of you."

Her praise filled him with a surprising amount of satisfaction. With graceful strides she moved passed him to examine her patient. The sweet scent of roses trailed behind her and her long braid left a damp line down the back of her yellow cotton shirt. Obviously she'd just returned from the bathhouse because she looked and smelled as fresh as a spring day.

His gaze traveled over her appealing

curves as she worked. Attraction surged through him, physical, yet so much more.

She was beautiful with that fiery red hair he longed to unbraid, her unselfish generosity to those around her was a treasure and her temperament challenged him in a way few other women had. Most of the women he'd dated over the years were more interested in looking good on his arm than having an intellectual conversation.

Everyone, that is, except Jenny.

Another failure against him.

His mother would have said it was his choice in women, not the women themselves, that was the problem. He knew that was true. Women who didn't hold his interest were safe, until they started wanting something more permanent. That was when he bowed out of the relationship without a backward glance.

But Gwen was different.

He'd like to get to know her better, find out why she seemed so disturbed when he came too close to her.

At first he'd thought it was just him, that

she found him unattractive or repulsive even, but he'd noticed she didn't allow any man to get physically close to her. And she didn't really give away many details of her childhood or her life before coming to his father's clinic.

Born and raised in Portland was all he knew. He wasn't used to women who didn't like talking about themselves. He knew more about Joyce than he wanted to and they'd only spent a minimal amount of time together.

Over the side of the child's bed she met his gaze, her amber eyes alight with question. "Derek, are you okay?"

"Uh, sure." He shook himself out of the trance he seemed to have fallen into. "Can I bring you some breakfast?"

"I've already eaten, thanks."

"I'll be right back then," he said and backed out the door.

Within a few minutes he was back with a plate of Matoke for James, who ate with relish.

Cam had fallen asleep again. Derek

could hear Gwen and the others talking in the hall, trying to decide where to move Cam so they could open the clinic. He joined them.

"How about putting Cam in my bunk," he offered.

"We've thought of putting him back here, but once we move him we shouldn't move him again until he's better," explained Gwen.

"He can have my bed as long as he needs. I'll camp out on the floor," Derek countered.

"You'd do that?" Gwen gazed up at him in surprise and approval.

"Yeah. It's not a big deal." He fought the urge to lean forward and kiss her smiling lips.

"Now I feel like a heel," complained Craig. "We could take turns sleeping on the floor."

"Speak for yourself," replied Ned.

Joyce gave a husky laugh. "Yeah, Ned needs his beauty sleep."

"You got it," he quipped back. Then he grinned. "Seriously, I'll sleep wherever."

"Then it's settled. We move Cam in our room and the guys will rotate bunks and floor," Derek declared.

Gwen surprised him by reaching out and squeezing his arm. "You're the best."

"Oooh, that's high praise," ribbed Joyce.

Gwen's cheeks grew red but she raised her chin and ignored the remark. "We should make the switch quickly then."

Derek carried Cam to his bunk and gently laid him down. Gwen propped Cam's leg up with a pillow and covered him with a blanket. Grandpa James hovered close by.

"Why don't you lie on one of the other bunks and rest now, James? We'll be just out front if you need anything," Derek said.

James's weathered face showed his appreciation in the tired smile he gave. Derek helped him to lie down.

He and Gwen left them to rest. In the hall she stopped and spun toward him. "You're a good man, Derek Harper."

Floored by her declaration, he arched a brow. "Was there some question about that?"

She grimaced. "Yes, actually. My first impressions of you weren't so hot."

"Now you think I'm hot," he joked with a grin.

Her eyes widened with dismay. "No, no. I just meant, you seemed arrogant and selfish and now I see compassion and kindness."

His good humor deflated like a balloon with a pinhole. "You were judging me before you knew me," he stated, enjoying the flustered way she scrambled to answer.

"I didn't mean to. It's just I'd heard so much about you before I met you. And I assumed because of the way you grew up, you'd be typically spoiled."

He stared at her. "The way I grew up?"

She had no idea how he'd grown up, always wanting his father's attention but no matter how many A's or trophies he brought home, Ross Harper barely spared his son more than a passing pat on the head.

That is, until Derek was older and his father realized that being friendly with the other dads on whatever team Derek happened to be on could bring new donors to Hands of Healing International.

Now that Derek had been in the field, so to speak, he understood the need, but it didn't erase all the years of wishing his father had time to shoot some hoops or play catch in the backyard.

Little creases appeared between her dark auburn brows. "I just meant—"

He held up a hand to cut her sentence short. "Don't sweat it. Hey, I'm a mama's boy through and through. I'm not ashamed. You better get out there to the masses."

She blinked and opened her mouth to say something but must have thought better of it because she spun away and quickly disappeared back into the clinic.

Derek grabbed his necessities for the bathhouse and went outside. The chatter of over a hundred people gathered around the clinic was oppressive and overwhelming. Derek's heart squeezed to think that all of those people had come from far places for the chance to have some care. He studied the faces as he passed through the crowd, seeing the signs he'd come to recognize as dehydration and illness.

The water!

He changed directions and went back to the spot where he'd left the jugs, but they were gone.

He walked all the way around the building thinking maybe someone had moved them out of the way. He went inside and asked if anyone had seen two jugs of muddy water sitting outside.

Gwen hurried to him. "What happened? What water are you talking about?"

"I opened the well and brought some water for you to test. I assume you have some way to make sure it's usable?"

"Yes, of course, we do. We need to find that water."

The concern shining in the irises of her eyes sent a thread of apprehension spiraling through him. "I'm sure it just got moved. I used the jugs from the bathhouse, so that's probably where they are. I'll go check."

She nodded. "Come back and let me know."

They weren't in the bathhouse. Derek headed to the kitchen on the off chance someone had stashed them there. He found the jugs, empty.

"Mya, where's the water that was in these?"

"I don't know." She asked the other women. One young girl stepped forward and explained how she'd found the water and had recently poured it into the boiling pot that they used to make the Matoke.

Derek's stomach dropped like a rock in the river. He never should have let the water out of his sight. Fearing someone else might have used them, also, he asked, "Were they still full when you found them?"

The girl shook her head. "One of the jugs wasn't all the way full."

A lump of dread formed in his throat. He took the remaining water from the kitchen and set the pot on the ground to cool. "Don't give out any more of that."

He ran to the clinic to tell Gwen, the

whole time berating himself for his reckless actions. He should have told Gwen or the others that he'd found the water in the well and had them test it before he brought any into the village. What if it was contaminated?

Oh, Lord, please don't let the water hurt anyone!

Gwen's face paled. "Ned, can you go?"

He nodded, grabbed a small white box from a cabinet and followed Derek out.

"Testing kit," he explained at Derek's questioning gaze. Ned took a small vial full of the water and then hurried inside.

Derek sank to the ground and propped his hand on his knees and hung his head.

Ned reappeared a moment later. "Harper, get in here."

Feeling like the scourge of the century, Derek got to his feet and braced himself to face the disappointment he was sure to see in Gwen's eyes.

"Okay, everyone, let's not panic," Gwen stated in as calm a voice as she could muster. Inside she was quaking. "How many people have ingested food made with the questionable water or drunk from the jug? Those are the first questions we need answered so we can be prepared for the worse-case scenario."

She looked around the room, seeing the same thought in every face that she'd had. Were any of them infected? They didn't even know yet what they were dealing with. For all they knew the water could be fine.

"What diseases do you think could have been in the water?" Derek asked, his voice shaky and his green eyes dark with self-recriminations.

She sought to reassure him as well as everyone else. "It could be anything or nothing. Let's not start off with the negative until we have to."

For Derek and the others not medically trained, she explained that several tests would be run on the water samples collected.

"If bacteria are present, they will produce hydrogen sulphide, which turns a treated paper slip black. This test can also indicate the severity of water contamination by the level of discoloration.

"Another test, the coliphage detection test, will indicate the presence of E. coli. This is often a sign that other dangerous bacteria, viruses or parasites transmitted by people may also be present. This test takes 8-24 hours of incubation."

"So what do we do in the meantime?" asked Craig, his worried eyes boring into her.

They were all looking to her for answers. She took a deep breath. Be prepared and you won't be vulnerable. "Preparation is key. We cut back on how much water and medicines we dispense until we know more. We certainly don't want to run out of meds if we have an outbreak of an infectious disease. We need to round up those who might be infected and observe them while we wait out the incubation period.

"For now we wait with a mindset to move fast if something appears. We don't want to start a panic with the people outside these walls, either. So be discreet in finding those who ate from the last batch of Matoke this morning and quarantine them…" She faltered. "Moses, ideas?"

"The church?"

She hadn't thought of that. The village church, built back in the eighties, was a brick structure with a low roof and lots of glassless windows. "Good. Ask Father Abram if we can use the building. We also need to find whoever drank directly from the jug. That person will probably end up the sickest if the water is contaminated. All right, everyone, let's get out there."

Gwen waited until everyone but she and Derek remained in the main room. He looked so dejected she didn't have the heart to scold him.

"I screwed up," he stated, squaring his shoulders.

She admired his sense of responsibility. Tenderness seeped through her, taking the edge off her panic. "Your heart was in the right place."

He shook his head. "No. It was selfish.

I wanted to be the hero, the good guy, and I ended up hurting people."

"We don't know that yet." She moved closer, just enough that she could touch his arm without feeling crowded. "It could turn out the water isn't contaminated."

He covered her hand with his big, warm palm sending little pleasant jolts up her arm to settle somewhere in the vicinity of her heart.

"When I first realized there was water in the well, I should have had you test the water there instead of bringing it here. I should never have just left it outside where anyone could get at it. I should have used my head."

His voice, so full of self-loathing, made her ache inside. "What's done is done. Berating yourself over it isn't going to help. You did what most anyone who wasn't a doctor would do. You can feel bad, but you didn't do anything to warrant guilt."

He curled his lip. "I should just leave for Kampala now and concentrate on what I do best."

"Running?"

"Yes. At least that won't hurt anyone."

She removed her hand and tried to force the rising irritation to stay out of her voice. "Sorry, Harper. You'll have to have your pity party later. You're not running off until we have a handle on this situation. I need you here."

"I should never have come. I knew it would be a disaster."

She studied him. "Why did you come?"

"Certainly not to cause problems."

"Look. Being prepared is half the battle. You're a problem solver, remember. We're going to need that. Now, go clean up." She waved him away.

He slanted her a glance, his lips twitching and she waited for some smart remark but none came.

She entered his domain with an attempt at teasing. "You do have a certain… aroma going."

That brought a small smile to his handsome face. "Thanks. I'll take care of that right away. But first I'm going to go check on Cam and James."

He spun away and disappeared down the hall.

Gwen wondered what he was running from. Odds were, Derek didn't know, either.

Chapter Nine

The next twenty-four hours were the
longest in Derek's life. Everyone was edgy
and tense. Only three people so far had
had a helping of the second batch of
Matoke and they hadn't found the person
who'd drunk directly from the jug. He
should have a big F attached to his
forehead. Failure chipped away at him,
bringing home his inadequacies.

The only solace was that Cam was
getting better with every passing hour. The
boy was lively and had a quick wit that
Derek enjoyed. The yearning to have a
child of his own caught him by surprise.

But he couldn't let his mind go there. He would never allow himself to be put in a position where he could cause disappointment and pain to a child.

Cam's grandfather told the story of how Cam's parents had died during a skirmish between Moswani's rebel forces and the Ugandan militia.

Derek had almost forgotten about the threat of the civil war since the village and clinic hadn't been affected thus far. But to the Africans, war, famine and disease were a way of life.

Little by little Derek was gaining a better understanding of the passion his father had for the country and its people. Those he'd met were kind and gentle with loving and generous spirits. It was a travesty that the modern world was so slow in sharing the fruits of its labor with underdeveloped countries.

It saddened him, as well, to learn that James was a rarity in that he was elderly. Gwen had explained that most people died before reaching old age, either from disease, war or injury. The reality of that seemed somehow harsher.

Few children had grandparents to spoil them with love. Derek couldn't fathom having gone through life without his grandparents. Both sets were still alive and he enjoyed the time he spent with them.

As Derek sat talking with Cam and James, hearing more about their lives, he decided that whatever money he gained from the upcoming race would be used to help Cam and James.

He didn't have his father's skills to help many, so he'd have to settle for helping a few.

He was telling Cam about seeing the Bonobo family when Gwen walked in. She stared at him for a long moment. Her expression was subdued even if her clothing wasn't. The shocking green velour top and matching bottoms contrasted with her red hair and pale skin and made Derek think of an elf at Christmas.

"You didn't tell me about that," she finally said with an edge of reprimand in her tone. "What if the monkey had felt more threatened?"

He'd meant to tell her, but had decided that doing so didn't serve his purposes but would only make her more crabby about his treks through the bush. "I didn't think you'd take it well. Obviously, I was right."

She pressed her lips into a tight line. "Ned's checking the culture if you want to come watch."

"I'm right behind you," he said while dread ate away at his stomach.

With dragging feet he followed Gwen. *Dear God, please don't let anything bad be in the water.*

Inside the clinic a group had gathered around to watch Ned as he examined the culture under the microscope. "Hhmm," he murmured.

"Well?" asked Joyce as she bobbed on her toes. Her agitation fed the tension filling the air.

Ned slid his gaze over the group and landed on Derek. "The strip's gray."

Around the lump lodged in his throat he asked, "Meaning?"

"Indicates some bacteria."

The news winded Derek like a short uphill sprint.

Ned's gaze shifted to Gwen. She toyed with her braid, her long graceful fingers combing through the feathered tail where the rubber band ended.

"There's coliphage present," Ned stated.

"E-coli?" Gwen asked in a hushed voice.

Ned shook his head. "More like cholera."

Derek sucked in a strangled breath. He recognized the name but didn't know anything about the disease other than it killed. Great, now he was a potential murderer. Could things get any worse?

Apparently they could. Tito arrived a few minutes later saying his cousin was sick and could a doctor please come. Derek's insides twisted. He knew how much Tito respected his cousin, who encouraged his running.

"I'll come," Gwen said shooting a quick glance at Derek.

His stomach knotted. *Please, God, let Al have a simple cold.*

Gwen took charge and spoke with efficiency. "Craig, you start getting the meds for cholera to the people over at the church."

"Will do," Craig said as he and Moses started gathering supplies.

"Ned and I will keep the clinic going," Joyce stated with a firm nod of her head.

"Thanks." Gwen grabbed her stethoscope and placed it around her neck. She took a small bag of supplies from a cupboard and headed outside. "We don't usually do house calls because we get so busy here," she said to Derek as they fell in step together. Tito had run on ahead.

"I appreciate that you're doing it now," he replied. He picked up the pace but kept his gait even and on the short side. He was impressed that she matched him stride for stride. She was an astounding woman and there was no one he wanted walking beside him more than her.

Even if he wouldn't ever say that out loud.

Ten minutes later they arrived at Tito's cousin's house, a mud structure with a thatched roof. On the small wooden porch sat two bamboo rocking chairs where Derek and Tito had sat many times in the last week.

Gwen paused at the door and handed him a mask. At his quizzical look she explained, "We don't know what he has yet. It may not have anything to do with the water."

He nodded and prayed that was so, then amended that prayer. Too much sickness prevailed on this continent.

Inside the house was stark but comfortable.

Al was older than Tito, burly and strong looking, except now he lay curled in a ball on his cot. He wore loose-fitting green pants and a T-shirt that had a sports logo Derek recognized. Al's insides were cramping and nothing wanted to stay in his body.

Al admitted that he'd taken a swig from one of the jugs of water when he saw

Derek put it down. He figured since Derek was with the clinic the water was safe.

Derek wished the ground would swallow him up right there as he explained where the water came from.

Gwen examined Al and said she'd have to go to the clinic and bring back water and medicine. The tenderness and compassion she displayed with Al moved Derek. He found himself hoping one day she'd treat him with the same level of care, and not because he was in a sickened state.

Whoa! Wait a minute. He shook that thought away. He wasn't even going down that trail.

Derek pulled up a chair. "I'll wait here," he said to her rather pointed look.

She gave a curt nod and left. An awkward silence descended. Al closed his eyes and moaned.

"Hey, man. I'm so sorry about this. I shouldn't have taken any water from the well," Derek finally said.

Al's pain-filled eyes regarded him. "You tried to help. No blame in that."

Tito put his hand on Derek's shoulder in agreement with his cousin. Derek appreciated their grace but guilt overflowed inside him making him feel ill.

Gwen returned a few minutes later with several bottles of drinking water and some pills. "Al, these pills will work to kill the cholera. You need to drink all of these bottles of water to flush the bacteria from your insides."

She nudged Derek out of the way and then placed a hand under Al's head and lifted him enough to take the pills with a gulp of water.

"Let the medicine do its job. Keep drinking. Tito will help you as you need."

She gave Tito instructions and then motioned for Derek to leave with her. He wanted to stay and keep Tito and Al company, but helping with the clinic took priority. He needed to work to redeem himself from this mess.

"Will he be well enough for the race next week?"

Gwen shrugged her slender shoulders.

"Hard to say. He's young and in good health. Plus, we caught it early."

Derek stopped walking. "Do you believe God hears your prayers?"

She halted to stare at him. "Yes. He hears all of our prayers."

"But He doesn't answer all of our prayers," Derek said as a little bubble of anger floated to the surface and materialized in his voice. He'd prayed for a father who would pay attention to him. That prayer went unanswered.

Contemplation shimmered in the gold of her eyes. "Everyone's prayers are answered. But not always in the way we want."

He frowned. "Then what good is prayer?"

Her eyebrows nearly reached her hairline. "Wait a second. God isn't some genie in a bottle that you pull out to grant your wishes. Life doesn't work like that. We make a request and He decides the outcome. But always it's for the good of those who love Him."

"I prayed that no one would get sick but Al still did."

Gwen could barely contain the warmth or the smile spreading through her. It was an odd yet pleasant feeling. She rarely got warm and fuzzy except when it came to children. Adults, especially younger, attractive men, left her cold.

She realized God had handed her an opportunity to help Derek understand Him. She sought for a way to tell Derek without preaching.

In her mind she saw her friend Claire and took a page from her book on how to talk to those whose hearts and minds were resistant to the Lord as hers had been all those years ago. God had seemed so far out of reach and not worth seeking. But Claire had talked with simple, straightforward truth.

And so would she. "God always answers. Sometimes yes, sometimes no. If we come to Him with our burdens, we have to trust He'll do what's best for us."

He shook his head, clearly confused. "But how does Al being sick help anyone?"

Here came the tricky part; trying to

explain a concept that had taken years for her to grasp. But she had to give explaining it a try, hoping that her words would bring him closer to God. *Give me the words, Lord.* "You care about Tito."

"Yes, he's a great kid."

"But you feel let down by God because Tito's cousin is sick."

A resentful shadow crossed his face. "I do."

She understood that emotion. Sometimes when she looked back at her childhood, she couldn't fight the bitterness that grabbed at her for what she'd gone through. Yet had it been different she wouldn't be the person she was today. "Everything happens for a reason. Sometimes God allows circumstance to come into our lives for the sole purpose of getting our attention so that we can see His hand at work and build our faith. Whether it's your faith or Al's or Tito's, I don't know.

"The book of James talks about rejoicing in trials, which is so against our human nature, but the trials we go through and the trials we witness in others help to teach us to trust God."

He didn't say anything for a long time. His gaze was directed out to the distant horizon but she sensed his focus was inward.

"Does that make sense?" she asked, feeling inept.

"It's a little hard to get my mind around the concept, but my father has said similar things." He clenched his fists. "I just wish there was something I could do to help right now."

"It would make you feel better if you could fix the situation. But maybe God wants you to trust Him to fix it."

"So trusting Him means we do nothing?"

"No. Our faith must be active."

He moved his hands in a wide arc that clearly showed his growing exasperation. "Which means…?"

"Which means, we do our part and let God do the rest."

"Okay. What is our part?"

She started walking. "That's what we have to figure out, Mr. Problem Solver."

He kicked a rock, sending it skidding into the bushes. "Great."

She smiled and tucked away the knowledge that maybe she would be able to fulfill her promise to Dr. Harper after all.

But would it be at the risk of losing her heart to Derek?

The next day, Derek and Moses drove the white van back to Kampala for the purpose of bringing back more water and a list of meds that Gwen had written on a sheet of paper now residing in the back pocket of Derek's lightweight khaki pants. The people they'd quarantined in the church had mild cases of cholera because the water had been diluted.

Gwen predicted they would be well within a few days as long as they continued with the medication and drank plenty of water to flush out their systems. Al, on the other hand, was still bedridden and miserable. The weight of guilt settled heavily on Derek's shoulders.

The long drive to the country's capital

looked much different than it had the night they'd arrived. Lush foliage lined the dusty, dirt road. They passed interesting huts and fields full of workers, both young and adult. People walked along the edge of the road, stepping off as cars whizzed by. Some held their hands up in greeting, others didn't acknowledge them as they stepped aside to keep from being run over.

At the checkpoints, people rushed to the car, hawking their wares—roasted pig on sticks, clay pots, figurines, fruit and vegetables. He and Moses waved the vendors away.

Kampala came into view, a concrete world looking out of place amongst the greener hills, yet reminiscent of most any other big metropolis. Tall buildings, a bit of hazy smog, the smell of diesel in the air all brought the city into focus.

The roadway became more congested the closer he and Moses drew to the city. Moses deftly maneuvered their vehicle through the traffic of battered cars, white-and-blue checkered taxis and pedestrians.

A roundabout spiraling off in several directions sat in the center of the main thoroughfare.

Derek hung on to the door handle as Moses swerved suddenly to the left, cutting in front of a jeep and barely missing a minibus's back bumper. Moses skillfully brought their van to a halt in a parking spot on a narrow strip of road in front of a row of shops.

"What an experience," Derek commented as he climbed out of the van. He'd thought Seattle's traffic problems were bad.

Moses grinned. "I've been driving since I was ten. I'm good, yes?"

"Very." Derek grinned back. He wondered about the life Moses had had growing up here. Driving at ten when he should have been playing sports and doing homework. "Did you go to school here in Kampala?"

Moses shook his head. "I attended four years of school in Masaka."

"Just four years?"

"I was lucky."

A twinge of disquiet settled in Derek's

soul. He, like most Americans, took their way of life for granted. Growing up, he'd considered school a chore, not a privilege.

Moses held out his hand. "Give me the list of supplies. I will go in and buy them."

Derek hung on to the list. "I'll come with you."

"No, no. You mustn't. If they see a *Muzungu,* they will double the price. And if they realize you're an American, the price will be four times the amount."

"Why would they do that?"

Moses shrugged. "It's Africa." As if that should explain everything.

Derek trusted Moses knew what he was talking about. He handed over the list. "Okay, I'll stay here."

Moses pointed to a newer-looking structure with many stories and lots of windows. "You might want to go there."

"What is it?" The view of the marquee was obstructed by a strand of trees.

"American hotel."

His reaction wasn't as strong as it would have been a week ago. "Sounds good. I'll meet you back here in an hour and then you'll take me to…"

He pulled out the papers that had the information about registering for the race. "To this address on Victoria Avenue."

"Yes. That won't be hard to find."

They separated. Moses disappeared into one of the stores and Derek walked toward the hotel. As he drew closer, he saw that the hotel was a Sheraton. A bit of home away from home.

As he walked in, it struck him that he could have been walking into the same hotel in any part of the world. The familiarity of the atmosphere was welcome, yet strange. He realized how accustomed he'd become to life in the village.

The rhythmic, steady pace, the feeling of community. Not so alone.

As he passed through the lobby and headed for the front desk, he recognized several runners he'd competed against in the past. One in particular snagged his attention and he veered toward where his old college classmate and fellow runner sat in a big, plush chair reading a news-paper.

"Hey, Owen," Derek called.

Owen Sparks looked up from the paper, his broad features breaking into a genuine smile. Owen stood, his hand outstretched. He wore pressed chinos and an oxford button-down that hung on his lean body. "Harper, you dog. I didn't know you'd be here."

They shook hands, each squeezing the other's hand in a friendly display of power.

"You racing next week?" Derek asked.

"Wouldn't miss it. The purse is good. You've never run this race, have you?" Owen peered at him, speculation plain in his light gray eyes.

"No," Derek admitted. He'd never been interested in running the longer dirt-trail marathons. He usually stuck with the more civilized road races. But his father had shown interest and talked up Africa, so here he was. And his father wasn't. Typical.

"It's grueling. Hot days, cold nights. No

comforts along the way." Owen grinned. "You'll love it."

"Yeah, we'll see. Where can I get a soda around here?"

"Follow me."

Owen led Derek to a small café in the hotel. They sat at a table by the window and ordered drinks. Though the glass buffered them from the hustle and bustle of the city, Derek found himself fascinated with the people.

He saw many pedestrians stop and chat with those they passed. Drivers waved at those on the street. Most of the people had smiles on their faces. Even in the city it seemed the African people were a good-humored lot.

"So where're you staying?"

Derek turned his attention to Owen. He hesitated for a moment, not sure he wanted to reveal too much about himself. But then he decided not to make a big deal about it. "I'm at a village a few hours drive from here. My father has a clinic set up there."

"Your father's here?" Owen said, breaking into an eager smile.

The familiar sensation of resentment bored into Derek. Like most of the people in Derek's life, Owen loved his father. And why wouldn't he? To most people, he was practically a saint, who went around helping the poor and healing the sick.

Just like Gwen.

Chapter Ten

Derek shook his head. "Dad broke his leg right before we left."

"Too bad."

"Yeah," Derek agreed, as shame replaced his resentment. He didn't like seeing his father laid low. "But the clinic is still going strong. My father put a competent woman in charge."

Owen raised his dark brows. "A pretty lady?"

"You could say that," Derek replied slowly, thinking that pretty was too mild a word to describe Gwen with her freckled nose and soul-searing eyes. "She has this natural beauty that knocks you off your feet. She's really amazing. She's really good with people and knows what she's doing even if she is a little young."

"Got a thing for her, huh?"

Derek blinked and a mental warning sign flashed through his brain. "What? No. Why would you say that?"

"Man, you can't kid a kidder. I can see it written all over your face."

Derek gave a dismissive wave of his hand. "She's not my type."

"Not a bubbleheaded babe like you favored in college?"

Derek chuckled. "You got that straight." Though he'd stopped dating that type of woman a long time ago. Now he favored…bossy redheads, a little voice inside his head whispered. He rolled his tense shoulders. *Not even.*

"Ah, well." Owen turned the subject to the race. "Have you paced out the route yet?"

"I don't do that. Ruins the mystery."

Owen gave an amused snort. "Right.

Well, it will definitely be interesting. This country has a lot of unrest on all fronts. I've been assured, though, that the race will be safe. The route along Lake Victoria will provide some great scenery."

"This is a beautiful country," Derek commented as he drank from his soda.

"That it is." Owen set down his coffee mug and stood. "Hey, man, it's been great to see you. I'm headed to Kenya for a few days. Going on a safari. Want to come?"

Derek shook his head, surprised that he didn't have any desire to take off. And even more surprised to realize he wanted to put work before his own pleasure. "No, I have to get back to the clinic. I'm needed there."

Owen looked surprised. "Cool. I'll see you in about four days at that starting line."

"And I'll see you at the finish line when you come in after me," Derek quipped.

"We'll see, man. We'll see." Owen waved and strode away.

Derek finished his drink and then walked back to the van. Moses was putting the bottled water into the back. Derek grabbed a jug in each hand and lifted them in. "Everything go smoothly?"

Moses paused and bobbed his dark head. "I bought all the items on the list and the water."

"Great, let's head out," Derek said as they both climbed in. Moses pulled out into the traffic. A horn blared as he darted between two cars and curved to the left, then shot down a side street. He wound the van along the street, dodging bikes and mopeds as well as cars.

He turned on to Victoria Avenue and found the address they were looking for. Derek climbed out and vaulted up the cement stairs of a squat building. A uniformed doorman behind a metal desk directed Derek to the third floor.

A line had already formed. Derek confirmed this was the place to register for the race.

He stepped in line and waited while chatting with those around him. An hour later, Derek stood before the woman processing the entrants.

With a weary smile the woman handed him a stack of paper and explained what needed to be done. He filled out the necessary forms and paid his entrance fee. He was given a number to attach to his running shirt, a water bottle with a sponsor's logo and paperwork explaining the route, complete with a map showing the checkpoints.

On the map he noticed that several rivers came off of Lake Victoria and spread through the countryside. One of those rivers had to be the one that had dried up. "Do you know anything about the rivers drying up?" he asked.

Her brown eyes turned sad as she replied, "The rivers are not dry. The military dammed them in an effort to make the rebels put down their weapons and surrender."

His heart kicked up speed. The river drying up wasn't a natural occurrence but man-made. And man-made things could be destroyed. There was hope for the villagers.

He asked the woman if she knew where the blockage in the water was and she indicated on the map the most likely location. After thanking the woman, he hustled back outside.

The priority was to get the supplies back to the clinic and then Derek vowed he'd find a way to get the water flowing. Even if he had to break down the dam with his own two hands.

He really looked forward to the smile on Gwen's face when he'd be able to tell her what he'd done.

"Where are you going now?" Gwen's shoulders tightened with exasperation, sending a dull ache up through her skull to settle in a pounding beat behind her eyes.

"I have something I have to do," Derek replied without even glancing at her as he walked toward the white van. In his hand he carried a small duffel bag she hadn't seen before.

"Something to do with your race?" She strove for a calm voice. She couldn't believe he was planning to take off again.

He'd seemed so much more focused since he and Moses had returned a few hours earlier. They'd unloaded the much-needed supplies and then Derek had gone to visit both Cam and Al.

He slanted a sideways glance at her. "No, something else."

She hurried in front of him, blocking his path. "We need you here."

"I'll be back," he said. His green eyes held some emotion in check that she couldn't identify.

She narrowed her eyes and wondered why he was so secretive. "Yeah, then you'll leave again for your race."

Running a hand through his sun-bleached hair, he said, "My race isn't for another four days. I'll be back in a few hours. Then you can boss me around to your heart's content."

Stung, she frowned. "I don't mean to boss you around. Your father put a lot of responsibility on me and I'm just trying to do a good job."

"You *are* doing a good job," he said with exaggerated patience.

Her heart did a little hiccup. He thought she was doing a good job?

"So why don't you go do your job over there and leave me to do what I need to," he added.

A prickling of apprehension held her in place. "Tell me what you're doing first."

He studied her face with his probing gaze for a beat. "Only if you promise to go back to the clinic."

"I don't make promises I'm not sure I can keep. Just tell me already," she bit out. Irritation heated her blood.

He sidestepped her and opened the driver's side door. After tossing the bag onto the passenger's seat, he turned to her. "When I was in Kampala, I found out the military have blocked the river to force the Moswani rebels to surrender."

"Blocked the rivers," she repeated numbly as her mind tried to grasp the significance of his words. "Well, that's just plain dumb. Do they realize how many innocent people are suffering? Not all of Moswani wants to break away from the government. These are peaceful people who just want to live happy, healthy lives. Something must be done."

She started to head to the clinic. "I'll contact the embassy and have them plead the Moswani's case before the Ugandan parliament…." She stopped as she realized Derek had slid into the van and shut the door. She hurried back to the vehicle and tapped at the window. He rolled it down. "Where are you going?"

He slanted her a hard glance. "To see what can be done about undamming the river."

Her lungs contracted with a mixture of fear and frustration. "Uh, no. You can't."

A stubborn and determined line accentuated his strong jaw. "Watch me," he said and started the engine.

Anger exploded. "I know you want to be the hero and save the day, but you can't. It's too dangerous and you're too reckless. We need to go through the proper channels."

A burst of hurt darkened the green of his

eyes. "The proper channels will take too long. We need to take action now."

The stony resolve in his expression told her there was no way she'd convince him otherwise. Stubborn, impulsive, pigheaded man!

But she couldn't let him go off alone. She could go get Moses or Ethan or one of the villagers to go with him.

But there was no time. He'd never wait.

So she ran around the front of the van and climbed into the passenger seat.

"Get out, Gwen," he ordered, his voice hard and demanding.

"No. If you're going then so am I," she stated firmly, though inside she was quivering with dread.

"You said it was dangerous." His forbidding stare challenged her to retract her statement.

"Exactly why I can't let you go alone. At least I'm familiar with the country and the people."

"You can't come with me. Get out."

She folded her arms over her chest and

mutely stared at him. She'd make it clear that unless he wanted to bodily throw her out, she wasn't budging.

He made a disgusted noise in the back of his throat before throwing the van into gear and taking off in a cloud of red dust.

"Do you know where we're going?" Gwen belatedly asked a little while later as the van bumped along the main road leading to Kampala.

"I've got a map."

Leaving one hand on the steering wheel and using the other to dig into his bag, he pulled out a map of the country. He held it out for her to investigate. She opened the folded map, noting the highlighted line which must indicate the route of the marathon.

She found the river leg that came off Lake Victoria and ran through Moswani and held it up for him to see. He nodded and took a right on to a less traveled road.

Soon they were leaving what little civilization there had been for a dirt path that cut through the lush, overgrown bush.

Spindly stocks of tall grass swayed merrily in the sun. A heron flew past and landed on a branch of a small, tangled tree.

Gwen held on to the bar above the door frame as she watched the scenery jiggle by. She didn't think Dr. Harper was going to approve of this jaunt, but at least she was with Derek and could keep him out of trouble.

They came to the edge of the dry river basin. A deep impression filled with dusty red dirt snaked through the yellowing brush. He slowed the vehicle to a halt.

Gwen glanced at him. The hard planes in his handsome face made her want to reach out to soothe him but she kept her hands to herself. She didn't have the skills to offer comfort. "What now?"

"Hang on," he said and stepped on the gas, shooting the van forward and into the dry gulch.

"See, you're reckless and *crazy*," she said while hanging on to the dashboard and the bar above her head. She bounced in her seat as the van ran over rocks and jarred through potholes.

"Do you have a plan?" she asked between bumps. She should have asked that question a few miles back, not that it would have done much good other than to prepare her for this roller-coaster ride.

He grinned. "Find the dam and break it down."

She groaned. Crazy *and* enjoying himself. Thankfully, all rebel activity had been reportedly contained at the border regions to the north and south. Though her stomach knotted and her nerves strained tight, she was drawn to his ability to let go of fear and be out of control.

They drove on for several miles, then suddenly they rounded a bend and Derek slammed on the brakes. She braced both hands on the dashboard to keep from flying through the window even as her mind registered the situation in front of them.

Armed men stood in a line across the gulch, their weapons raised and their dark faces menacing. Fear flooded through her veins and panic sent her pulse skyrocketing. These men weren't Ugandan soldiers. So much for accurate reports. "Rebels!" she choked out.

Derek yanked the gearshift in Reverse, but only went a yard before stopping again. Gwen turned around to see that more men had blocked the way behind them.

One look at the grim expression on Derek's face sent another wave of panic straight to her head, making her dizzy.

"Just stay calm," he muttered as the men outside the van closed in. Derek rolled down his window. "Hey, man. We're lost. Can you point us toward the nearest town?"

If Gwen hadn't known Derek, she'd have thought he sounded like a normal tourist in a normal situation. But the knuckles of the hand that held the steering wheel turned white, while his other hand hovered over the gearshift. Did he plan to run them over? She couldn't allow that.

She leaned forward, needing to better

explain who they were. She was sure that once the men realized she and Derek were harmless, they'd back off. "I'm with the Hands of Heal—"

A man moved to her side window and banged on the glass. She yelped at the sudden intrusion and scooted closer to Derek. What had she been thinking to come with Derek on this foolhardy task? She should have dragged him out of the van instead of getting in with him.

"Out of the car," a big, imposing man boomed in a gruff voice.

"We'll just go back the way we came," Derek stated, his voice even. "If you could just have everyone move back."

The man raised his menacing gun and shoved it next to Derek's nose. Gwen's heart stalling, she clutched at Derek's arm.

"Hey, man. We don't want any trouble."

"Out!"

Having no choice, Derek opened the door. His hand closed firmly around Gwen's fingers as they slid out of the van. He kept her between him and the van. If the situation weren't so dire, she would have appreciated the protective gesture, but as it was, all she could think was they were doing to die. Right here in the middle of a dry river out in the bush.

She silently sent up a prayer for help and wondered how her life had gotten so out of control. "We're doctors with Hands of—"

"Quiet!" the big man shouted.

She hadn't felt this vulnerable since she was young and at the mercy of someone bigger and stronger.

A man sidled up from the left side, grabbed her by the arm and jerked her away from Derek. She screamed as her hand was ripped from Derek's. Jarring pain shot up her arm from the man's tight grasp. Tears welled behind her eyes and she blinked to keep them from forming.

Derek rushed forward to protect her. The big man who'd spoken hit Derek on the side of the head with the butt of his gun. Horror turned the world red as Gwen watched Derek crumble to the ground. "Derek!"

She twisted and bucked trying to get free. More rough hands grabbed at her. Her mind turned inward and more terror galvanized her struggle.

Memories of another time when rough hands had captured her tore through the protective barriers she'd put up to enable her to forget.

She fought the men holding her now with the same passion she'd fought all those years ago. She'd lost then, she prayed she didn't this time.

Her feet lashed out, her head thrashed. Her screams reverberated in her head.

Suddenly, the world exploded in sparks of pain on the side of her head. As her body rushed to meet the ground, she caught one last glimpse of Derek, saw blood seeping down the side of his handsome face and anguish filled her soul.

Then all went black.

Chapter Eleven

Derek's head pounded. He felt off-kilter and unbalanced. He was slumped over, his arms pulled tightly behind him, his body supported by ropes and the back of another warm body. He raised his head. The world swirled then righted itself and his stomach lurched.

Slowly he opened his eyes and blinked rapidly, his vision adjusting to the night. He was on the ground in a clearing surrounded by deep, dense foliage. Overhead the moon's glow hid behind clouds. There seemed to be no one else around.

For a moment his muddled brain struggled to comprehend where he was and what had happened. Then recollection slammed into him.

Gwen!

They'd been taken prisoner by armed men. They didn't wear uniforms like the Ugandan soldiers at the airport, so he surmised the men holding them were Moswanis.

Twisting around as best he could, he saw Gwen leaning limply to the side, her arms tied behind her back and her body kept from the ground by the same ropes holding him upright. He moved his hand and found her chilled fingers.

A spasm of fear contorted in his chest. She had to be alive.

"Gwen!"

A low moan answered him. Relief rushed through his bloodstream and the world spun again.

He used his shoulder to nudge her. She moaned again. He knew the exact moment she came fully awake. She stiffened away from his back and pulled on the ropes. He sensed her panic even though he couldn't see her face.

"Careful," he admonished gently.

She stilled. "Derek?"

"Here." He squeezed her hand. He expected her to relax back against him. She didn't. Her hand stayed limp in his. "Gwen?"

She didn't answer. He twisted to see her, his shoulders screaming in protest. "Look at me," he ordered.

Slowly, she turned her face toward him. The dull shock in her amber eyes tore at his soul. Questions flooded his mind. How long had he been out? What had they done to her? He couldn't bear the thought of those men laying their hands on Gwen.

Fury boiled in his veins. He blamed himself for the predicament they were in. If he'd just listened to her and let the proper people handle the situation, Gwen would be safe at the clinic. He'd let his need to prove himself, to be the hero, rule his head. Again.

He was always doing that. Rushing forward instead of proceeding with caution.

He could hear his father's voice warning him that one day his wildness would land him in trouble. He'd tried so hard to prove his dad wrong. Failure twisted his stomach into a ball.

Derek couldn't change who he was any more than he could make his father proud of him. Could he?

"Gwen, listen to me. We have to work together to find a way out of this."

Her eyes slid shut and her head bobbed forward.

"Gwen," he said, his voice sharp with anxiety.

She once again lifted her head and opened her eyes. Her gaze had cleared some. She blinked. "I think I'm going to be…" She threw herself forward, taking Derek backward with her as she dry heaved several times.

Pain jerked through Derek's shoulders and head. He ignored it, his mind flooded with concern for her.

"Get off me," she ordered as she tried to straighten, her movements pulling the ropes tighter.

"I can't," he huffed while struggling to right himself. "If you haven't noticed, we're tied together."

"Oh." She settled down. "You're right. Sorry." She twisted toward him, her eyes clearer and steady. "You were bleeding. Are you okay?"

He could feel something caked and sticky on his face, now he knew what it was. "Yeah. But not to worry, I've got a hard head."

"That's for sure," she muttered.

He smiled, glad to hear some spunk in her voice. His smile faded as concern grew in his chest. "Can you tell me what happened? Did they…hurt you?"

"I…I don't know." He could feel her shake her head, then heard her groan. "I was hit on the head, too. But other than that, I don't think so."

Small consolation that all they did was hit a defenseless woman. Rage chomped through him and he clenched his fist. "I'm so sorry, Gwen. This is all my fault."

"Not entirely. I should have made you stay."

He shook his head. "You couldn't have."

"I could have tried harder."

Self-recrimination squeezed his throat. "I should have forced you out of the van."

"You couldn't have," she echoed back.

"Yeah, well." He still felt guilty for putting Gwen in danger. She deserved better than this. He hadn't heeded her wisdom. "You don't have to sit so straight. Lean on my back."

There was a moment of silence. A chilly breeze caused his skin to prickle.

"Gwen?" Had she passed out again? Worry gnawed at his insides.

"I don't like to be touched," she said softly, her voice shaky.

"What?" That didn't make sense. The woman was a healer. He'd seen the way she used her hands with compassion as she tended to patients.

"It's an old issue," she added in a dismissive tone that surprised him and left him curious what she was hiding. But now was not the time to delve deeper, if ever.

"Gwen, listen to me. We're going to need to keep each other warm and with you sitting up so straight, the ropes are really cutting into my middle."

Ever so slightly she eased back, and the tension on the rope lessened. "Better?" she asked.

"Keep leaning."

She did until their backs were pressed firmly together. "Now, that's more like it. Are you warmer?"

"Yes. Thanks."

His hands sought hers; she stiffened again. "Relax, I want to see if I can loosen the rope."

"Where do you think they went?" she asked.

"I don't know and I hope we're not here when they come back."

Twisting his hand and bending his fingers, he worked at finding the knot. He felt Gwen trying, their skin brushing against each other's, a soft reprieve from the cutting rope.

"I can't get it."

Her frustration echoed in each word and mirrored his own growing aggravation. "We can't give up."

"No, we can't."

"What was that you'd said about trials being a joy?" He winced as the ropes rubbed his wrist raw.

"I didn't explain it very well if that's what you thought I said."

Her voice held a note of pain that slashed through him. He wanted to comfort her, protect her. But he couldn't and he loathed himself for that.

"We don't rejoice in the trials themselves but in the results trials produce," she said.

"This is one trial I'd rather have skipped, because I don't see anything productive about it."

She gave a dry laugh. "As God keeps reminding me, we are not in control."

Something wet and warm ran down his fingers. "Stop."

"What?"

"One of us is bleeding."

"I felt that, too. But I don't know if it's me or you."

"Me, neither." Derek tilted his head in defeat. There was no way they were going to get out of this. He got her into this. Add another screwup to the list. "You better start praying."

"Don't you think I have been?"

"Do you think He is listening?"

"Yes. Yes, I do."

Her quiet assurance touched him and he sent up his own silent plea for help. They sat like that for a long time. The night sounds lulled his senses. Maybe it was the loss of blood or the blow to the head, but he found himself drifting off. He jerked awake. He had to stay alert and be ready for any opportunity to escape.

"You asleep?" he asked.

"Hardly."

"If we get out of this alive, my dad is going to kill me."

She gave a soft scoff. "I doubt it. He'll rejoice that you're safe."

"And give me a lecture on my impulsive behavior."

"Could you blame him if he did?"

He tested the ropes binding his feet. "No. This time it would be completely deserved."

"Since we're tied up here and you can't run away from me, I want to know why you are working for Hands of Healing?" she asked quietly.

He groaned. "Not this again."

"Humor me, okay? Distract me from the circumstances. You at least owe me that."

He scoffed slightly. "I didn't figure you for the guilt-trip type."

Her shoulders rose against his. "Whatever works."

"It's no big deal. Dad paid for school in exchange for a year's commitment to Hands of Healing."

"I knew something hinky was going on," she said after a pause.

"Did you now?"

"I sensed the tension between you and

your dad. I guess you resent his conditions."

"No. What I resent is that no matter what I do, it's never enough."

She turned her head and spoke over her shoulder. "Meaning?"

"Hey, we're your typical American dysfunctional family. Workaholic father, overcompensating mother and insecure kid. Enough said."

"There are a lot of people in this world who dream of having a family like yours."

He winced at the censure in her tone, feeling small. "I know that, Gwen. I'm not a complete idiot."

"I didn't say you were an idiot. I just think you're—"

"Immature, spoiled, afraid of commitment. Believe me, you wouldn't be the first woman to say that."

"They must not have known you very well then. You're one of the most committed people I've met."

Her praise sent an unexpected jolt of

pleasure through him. "Are you nuts? I don't do commitment."

"You're the one who's nuts if you believe that. It takes a lot of commitment to get through school. To train for and run a marathon. Repeatedly. You made a commitment to your father and you're honoring it. I'd say you do commitment just fine."

Her words rang with truth that he couldn't deny. So he amended his statement. "I don't do relationships."

"Why not?"

"Afraid of commitment," he stated smugly, even though she'd just pointed out that wasn't the issue.

"Ha! That's a cop-out."

He grinned at the sliver of moon visible behind the clouds. "Maybe. But it works."

"You're afraid, but it's not commitment that scares you."

"Oh, really? Care to share with me my phobias, Dr. Phil?"

Her chuckle sent a ribbon of warmth curling over him. He really liked her laugh. He liked her bravery and her steadfast faith. Face it; there was a lot to like about the woman.

"Have you ever had a girlfriend?"

He snorted. "I certainly haven't lived like a monk."

She nudged him with her shoulder. "A long-term girlfriend?"

He contemplated the shadows and thought about Jenny. She'd been blond, blue eyed and dimpled. A sweet, down-home girl who wanted picket fences and an attentive husband. "Yeah."

She turned her head toward him. "Why'd you break up?"

He closed his eyes against the memory of Jenny's hurt-filled blue eyes. "We didn't want the same things in life. There was no point in continuing on."

"You mean marriage?"

"Marriage, kids, the whole shebang."

"How long were you together?"

"Six months."

"That's not very long."

He shrugged. "Long enough for me to know she wanted forever."

"What's wrong with forever?"

A restless need to do something nagged at him. He ignored her question and worked his fingers at the ropes again.

After a moment, she let out a small scoff. "I think you're afraid to let anyone get too close."

"Thus the fear of commitment," he stated baldly.

"No. It's deeper than that. You're afraid if anyone really got to know you they wouldn't like the real you."

The arrow of her words shot him smack dab in the chest. His lungs contracted from the impact. "Look who knows so much," he quipped.

"You do that any time you get uncomfortable with the conversation."

"Do what?" he asked his voice full of fake skepticism.

"Give a smart remark or pick a fight."

Annoyance at her assessment converged in his head and made the ache behind his eyes pound that much harder. "You know, we should get some sleep so we have energy for whatever happens tomorrow."

"See, there you go, sidestepping because you're uncomfortable. What is it you're running from?"

Her perceptiveness was a real bothersome trait. "Why do you think I'm running from something? Maybe I'm running toward something."

"Okay, I'll bite. What do think you're running toward? What drives you to run races, to run from sticky conversations, from relationships?"

"Why don't you tell me why you don't like to be touched?" he asked, veering the conversation away from himself.

"We're not talking about me," she said sharply.

"Let's." She was coming way too close to the truth.

"Let's not. I think getting some rest is a good idea."

"Ha! Hypocrite!" She was playing his own game and he silently applauded her for that.

She didn't respond right away. He took a deep breath, thankful she'd let the subject drop. Delving into his psyche wasn't a favorite pastime. He didn't want to examine the reasons he was the way he was.

He knew he wouldn't like the answers.

"Fine. You want to know why I don't like to be touched?" she shot at him.

Her belligerent tone sent ripples of apprehension down his spine. "Yes."

Her fingers went rigid against his.

After a long pause, she said in a hoarse whisper, "I was raped when I was twelve."

Chapter Twelve

Behind her Derek stiffened on a hissed intake of breath. Gwen closed her eyes tight and wished her hands were free to cover her face. Just saying the words aloud brought shame flushing through her. Maybe the blow to the head had knocked a screw loose?

"I…I don't know what to say," he said softly, his voice full of concern, which she appreciated way too much.

"There's not much for you to say. You asked why I don't like to be touched. That's why."

"What…I mean, how did it happen?"

She opened her eyes and stared at the dark shadows so like the ones lurking in her soul. She didn't allow herself to go to that place.

She'd broken down once and told Claire, half-afraid she'd throw her out, but Claire had cried with her and told her that God had cried, too.

That had begun the healing process for Gwen and had softened her heart toward God to the point that she finally allowed Him into her heart and started to live for Him.

Before then, she'd felt dead inside.

She hadn't expected to ever reveal her past to Derek, but he had such a defensive barrier up that somehow she knew that the only way he'd let it come down was if she let hers down first.

A scary and difficult thing to do. She only hoped that it would do some good.

The sentiment from a contemporary Christian song ran through her mind. Something about not truly loving until you give your love away. The same could be said of trust.

As hard as it was going to be, she had to give of herself in order for Derek to give of himself, in order to heal him. Trust was earned. She prepared herself for the pain she knew would be inevitable as she relived that awful night.

"My parents died when I was ten. A drunken driver crossed the center line and hit them head-on."

She could still remember the police officer's expression as he came to the house to tell her. His dark face held such compassion and grief. Her babysitter, Mrs. Morse, had cried uncontrollably. Gwen wished she had been able to cry, but her whole being had gone into a numbed shock.

"I'm so sorry," Derek said and he gave her fingers a squeeze.

"I didn't want to believe they were gone. Even after I went to live with my aunt and uncle and their son, I kept expecting my parents to show up and take me home."

The desolate and deep pain of loss still clung to her, coloring her words with sadness.

"At least you had somewhere to go," he said softly.

She closed her eyes as bitter hate gathered at the corners of her mind. *Take it away, Lord. Please take it away.*

"That's what everyone said. I should be grateful to my father's sister for inviting me to live with them. But they took me in because it was the right thing to do, not because they had any affection for me. They were strict and fair for the most part except when it came to their son. Lloyd could do no wrong. On the honor roll, a star athlete. The Golden Boy."

His voice held a dark, raw note of anger. "How old was your cousin?"

"Five years older. For two years, he teased and tormented me. My aunt would tell me not to be a crybaby and to stay out of Lloyd's way. Never once did she or my uncle take my side even when it was obvious he'd done something nasty, like spilling his drink all over my homework or taking the garbage can and dumping it in my closet. Just stupid mean things." Rage clenched a steely fist around her insides.

"What happened when you were twelve?" he rasped.

She swallowed back the bile that rose. Her heart started beating faster. "The week before I turned twelve, Lloyd cornered me in the upstairs hall and tried to kiss me. I told Aunt Bernice and she slapped me." The sound of her aunt's hand hitting her cheek had rung in her ears for weeks.

"What a witch!"

"Yeah, well. You asked how I learned to punch, well I learned quickly how to keep Lloyd at bay. He would laugh and taunt me that I couldn't hurt him. So I practiced, lifting my uncle's weights when no one would notice. I started to hurt him.

"He tried to hit me back once, but his father had stepped out of his study in time to see him with his fist raised. Uncle Jarrod had raised a brow at Lloyd but that was all. Luckily it was enough to keep Lloyd from hitting me."

"Did you tell anyone?"

"Who was I going to tell? And who'd believe me?" She sighed as she forced herself to swallow back the acid that churned in her stomach. "Later that summer they all went away for a week to their cabin house and left me home alone."

Derek made a disgusted noise. "That's neglect."

"I didn't mind. When they were gone I was safe. I was self-sufficient enough to cook mac and cheese and hot dogs. And I didn't have to be on guard all the time. But then one night a bad storm hit and Lloyd came home. He'd said his parents wanted him to check on me."

"Oh, man," he ground out, dread lacing those two words.

She figured he guessed where she was headed, but she had come this far—she couldn't stop now. The need to tell him rose, oppressive in its intensity. "I was in my room when I heard the front door open. I thought they were all back so I wasn't real worried until Lloyd opened my bedroom door."

She shuddered at the memory of his wild-eyed look. "He reeked of alcohol. I ordered him to leave. He just laughed. This crazy sound that made the hairs on my arms stand on end. He came at me with this leering grin and even at that young age, I knew what he wanted to take from me. I fought him, threatened to tell his parents, to tell the police. He jeered at me, saying who'd believe the poor little orphan girl."

Hot tears ran down her cheeks, but she could only let them fall as her words tumbled out into the dark night. "After he left, I managed to clean myself up and then I grabbed everything I could carry, stole my aunt's cookie jar money and ran because I knew he'd come back and do that to me again. And there was no one who could protect me."

"Ah, baby, I'm so sorry that happened to you."

The thick emotion in Derek's voice brought fresh tears streaming down her face.

"Where did you go?"

She sniffed and took a deep breath, forcing herself to continue even as the shame tightened and bound her like the ropes holding her hostage. "I became one of the nameless, faceless teens living on the streets. I begged, borrowed, stole. I ate out of garbage cans or in soup kitchens. I bartered my body and my soul. I did what I had to in order to survive. To forget. Then one day two angels rescued me."

"Angels rescued you?" he said skeptically.

The sun was beginning to rise, spreading light with gentle strokes that painted the morning sky in vibrant pinks and oranges. Gwen watched the sky awaken and remembered.

"They weren't really angels, not the winged, haloed variety, anyway. I was pretty drugged out. This was before meth became so popular. Cocaine was my drug of choice. I had settled in a doorway in downtown Portland to ride a high when the door opened behind me. I fell back and smacked my head. In my state of mind, I thought I died or something when I looked up and saw these two beautiful women staring at me.

"That was the day I began to live again. The women, Claire and her aunt Denise, took me to live with them. No questions, no conditions. Just love. I was such a mess and such a royal pain in the beginning. But they were patient and kind. Then Aunt Denise got sick. I think Claire needed me as much as I needed her then. When Denise died, Claire and I became each other's family."

"Amazing."

"Very amazing. Claire and Aunt Denise showed me God's love through their love. Jesus said to love your neighbor as yourself. I think if everyone on earth practiced that there'd be less heartache in the world."

"Amen to that," Derek said.

"Claire runs a shelter for teen runaways. I was her first. I helped her with the others as I got older. It was gratifying to see these kids growing and changing. And some reconciled with their parents."

"How did you get into medicine?"

Feeling less vulnerable now, she said, "I'd always done well in school and wanted some way to help others. I thought about becoming a full-fledged doctor but decided Physician's Assistant worked because its less of the business part and more doctoring."

"But with what you went through and the way you've not wanted to be touched, isn't working with people difficult?"

She gave a little laugh. "Well, the things is, I'm in control of the touching. That I can handle."

She could feel him nodding. "That makes sense. I—"

A rustling in the bushes echoed in the stillness. Suddenly a dozen or so men emerged from the dense foliage, the same men who'd taken them prisoner. All of them held automatic machine guns.

The big man who'd struck Derek stepped close and squatted down. His dark eyes hard and probing. "What are you doing here?"

"I told you, we took a wrong turn. We're not here to cause any problems."

"You are a problem. People will come looking for you." The man stood.

The taste of fear was bitter in Derek's mouth. "Hey, if you just let us go, we won't tell anyone we even saw you."

"Bring them," the man ordered before once again disappearing through the bushes.

The command sent men scrambling over to where they sat. With rough movements, the men unbound them from each other and forced them to stand. The prolonged inactivity in the position of being bent at the knees made Derek's legs wobble.

Two men had to half drag him forward. Derek craned his neck to see Gwen. She, too, seemed to be struggling to stand on her own. He could see the distress in her sweet face and the tears on her cheeks as the men pulled her along.

He knew how much this was hurting her. He couldn't imagine the horror she was reliving. His heart ached from the pain of her story and he wanted to lash out. But some instinct kept him from recklessly acting on the impulse.

They moved through the undergrowth, branches scraping the bare skin of Derek's legs and arms. For several yards they continued on until they broke through to a clearing. Derek stared at the sight of the large blockade erected in the middle of the river. Water lapped at the wood-and-stone structure on one side while the sun baked the dusty earth on the other. What horrible irony that their captors had brought them to the place they'd set out to find.

It wasn't the government who'd deprived the villagers from the precious water source. But why would the rebels do this to their own people?

He and Gwen were unceremoniously deposited in a heap by the wet side of the riverbed. Derek met Gwen's terror-filled gaze as one man fondled her long braid.

"Leave her alone!" Derek yelled, his heart slamming into his throat.

The man's grin was cruel as he pulled

Gwen to him, her bound hands the only defense she had against his larger body. The other men gathered about to see the show.

"No!" Derek thrashed against his own restraints. Pain exploded in his shoulder as another man hit him with the butt of his weapon. It would take more than the butt of a gun to stop him from trying to protect her. But the restraints held no matter how much he fought them.

The man tried to press his mouth to hers. She resisted, her head thrashing side to side. Her legs gave out, though Derek wasn't sure if by design or fate, forcing the man to let her go. She crumpled in a heap on the ground and swiftly scuttled away from the captor above her. There were jeers and laughter at the man for being bested by the *Muzungu* woman.

"No, you don't," the man barked as he made a grab for her braid.

"Enough!"

The shouted command stilled everyone. Derek turned to see the leader approaching, his tall, lean body menacing and in control.

Gwen scooted as close to Derek as possible. Her body trembled against him. Softly she began to sing a praise song. Her normally clear voice was reedy and high. The leader frowned at her before marching past. The men followed him with suspicious glances at Gwen and gathered in a circle several feet away.

Gwen's voice grew stronger, her gaze bright and wild. Derek was sure she was cracking up. The stress of their capture and the mauling had been too much. Guilt ate at him like acid. He moved to position himself so she could lean on him. She did so as she sang, the words washing over him in a cascade of soothing sound.

He was so impressed and proud of her for the way she'd overcome her traumatic and painful childhood to become the fascinating woman he'd grown to care for.

And he did care for her in ways he'd never cared for anyone else. She was strong yet so vulnerable. Intelligent and loving. She challenged him, made him want to be more than he ever dreamed he could be.

He prayed that he'd get a chance to be that man.

Listening to the song of worship brought peace to his soul and he joined his voice to hers. Awareness of the stares directed their way made him sing that much louder. The group of men returned their attention to their leader, then dispersed.

The leader and four men, one of whom was the man who'd grabbed Gwen, disappeared upstream while several others vanished into the thick stand of trees. Two men stayed behind, presumably as guards.

Derek kept his eyes on the two men as they conversed. The taller of the two men lit a cigarette and leaned against the thick support pole of the dam. His dark pants and dark shirt hung loosely on his thin frame.

The other man wore his mean-looking weapon strapped over his body. He had on green army fatigues and a matching vest over a white T-shirt.

The men were too far away for Derek to hear their conversation, which in turn meant they wouldn't be able to hear him and Gwen. He stopped singing. "Gwen. Gwen."

The song she was singing faded.

"You okay?" he asked, concerned by the pallor of her skin and the dazed look in her eyes.

She took a deep breath and slowly let it out. "I guess. I'm scared."

"Me, too. But I'm choosing to believe what you told me earlier."

She blinked and raised an eyebrow.

"God's in control." Just saying those words released some of the tension in his chest, despite the gravity of the situation.

She nodded and leaned her head against his shoulder. He closed his eyes against the raw affection and tenderness slicing through the protective covering that surrounded his heart. She'd bared her soul to him, trusted him with her story and now had given him the greatest gift by allowing herself to find comfort in his closeness.

He was moved to pray as he'd never prayed before. As they sat there for the longest time, her head resting on his shoulder, their sides pressed together offering mutual support, he prayed. Silently at first, then under his breath, the words tumbling out as he raised his voice.

He asked God for forgiveness for his disbelief, for his resentment. He prayed for protection over Gwen and himself, for Cam and Tito and Al. For all the people at the clinic and the village. He prayed for the souls of the men who'd taken them captive. He asked for forgiveness on their behalf, for mercy to fall on them.

Gwen, too, began to pray aloud, their words mingling.

"Shut up!"

Derek's eyes jerked open. Gwen grew quiet, her body going rigid beside him. The short man loomed over them, his obsidian gaze angry, his face in a feral grimace.

In defiance, Derek spoke directly to the man. "May God forgive you and help you to find compassion in your soul."

The man jerked his weapon from around his body and raised the end up over Derek. "You'll see God soon enough."

The man swung the weapon and connected with the side of Derek's head. The world imploded in a shower of painful sparks. He heard Gwen scream. Derek's head hung forward and he forced himself to raise his chin to stare defiantly at the guard. "My God's stronger than you are."

The man's face twisted with rage. He raised his weapon again, his intent clear as he pointed the barrel at Derek's head.

"Stop!"

The shouted command came from a few yards away. The two guards aimed their weapons toward Cam's grandfather, James, Moses and Ethan as they came into view.

Derek groaned. Now more people were in danger because of his impulsiveness.

Would this nightmare ever stop?

James held up his hands and walked forward. He spoke in Swahili as he approached the men. Confusion crossed the guards' faces. Amazingly they lowered their weapons and stepped back. Moses and Ethan rushed forward.

"I'm so glad to see you," Derek stated. "How did you know where to find us?"

Moses untied the ropes wound around Derek's wrists and pulled him to his feet. "I heard you and Miss Gwen arguing before you left. When you didn't return, we set out to find you."

Ethan helped Gwen to her feet.

"Thank you, Ethan," she said and wobbled.

Derek slid an arm around her waist and supported her even though his own legs felt rubbery. James kept speaking as Moses and Ethan led Derek and Gwen down the dry riverbed to where a dark green ~~jeep wai~~ted. At the wheel of the jeep was Tito.

They all climbed in and within a few moments James joined them. Derek sat in the back with his arm protectively around Gwen. She snuggled close. Soon they were speeding down the dry riverbed and onto the dirt road taking them back to the clinic.

"What did you say to them?" Derek asked James.

He grinned. "I tell them you saved my grandson's life."

"Why would that matter?"

"In Africa when one does a good deed it is rewarded by all. We have a saying here, *Harambee*. It is a Swahili word meaning 'pulling together.' We must all do our part. I explained that you are with the clinic that is giving care to our people and you are needed."

"Wow, that's awesome." If only that concept worked in America. "I can't begin to tell you how thankful we are you all showed up," he said with heartfelt sincerity. His heart swelled with gratitude to God for the timely rescue.

He glanced at Gwen and saw that her eyes were closed and her breathing even. She'd fallen asleep with her head resting against his chest. He bent to place a light kiss on her hair.

An anxious ripple rolled through him. He didn't know what the future held for them, but a bond had formed between them and it was more frightening than staring down the barrel of a gun.

Gwen awoke as the jeep pulled to a stop. She became aware of the rhythmic sound of Derek's heart beating beneath her cheek. Suddenly shy and awkward, she sat up. He removed his arm, leaving her feeling vulnerable and out of sorts.

She hadn't prepared herself for the aftermath of revealing her past to him. Nor had she been prepared for the way she'd turned to him for comfort.

It had felt so good to have him beside her when she'd been so afraid. His touch was safe and that was amazing to her.

Now as they disembarked from the jeep and were engulfed by the people waiting for them, she only had a fleeting moment to wonder how she and Derek would relate now that they were back, before Joyce and Mya were crying with relief and hugging her tight.

The rest of the afternoon went by in a

haze of emotion as they told the story of their ordeal and relived the harrowing moments. Derek stayed far from her, his gaze once or twice touching on her before moving away. She didn't understand the subtle distance she felt emanating from him. Had she been wrong to confide in him?

No, she decided. She wouldn't begrudge telling him. Even if he didn't reciprocate her trust, she'd made a huge leap in letting herself talk about the past.

The sense of freedom she felt was worth the price of risking her heart.

She nearly groaned aloud at that thought. It figured. She'd finally allow herself to care and the man would be even more closed off and guarded than she was. What a sad state of affairs.

But at least they were alive and she was sure his faith had grown. She was pretty sure her promise to Dr. Harper had been fulfilled. And really, what more could she ask for?

Tired and sore, she finally broke away to go lie down. Tomorrow would be soon enough to get her life back on track. As she drifted off to sleep, she heard Derek's soothing voice whispering, "Good night, Gwennie."

She knew then what else she could ask for: to heal his wounded heart.

Chapter Thirteen

"Hey, Harper, wait up!"

Derek pivoted and his heart lurched at the sight of Gwen striding toward him. Her long red braid hung over one shoulder, her bright amber-colored eyes shone like jewels in the morning sunlight. She wore clean khaki shorts and a pink polo-style shirt.

The bandages on her wrists were the only sign of their ordeal, though he didn't doubt she sported a headache, as he did. The determined set of her mouth claimed the boss lady was back in charge.

"Good morning, Gwen. I'm headed to see Tito's cousin. Care to join me?"

Her expression softened with a smile. "I'd like that."

Boss lady turned friend? He liked it.

They walked through the village, waving hello and calling out greetings. They entered Al's house to find him and Tito sitting at the table eating their breakfast. Tito smiled and Al rose and slowly came to them. "Mr. Derek. Miss Gwen. I'm so happy to see you!"

"You're looking better," Gwen said as she reached to take his pulse.

"I'm glad to see you up and about," Derek replied and gave Al a hug as Gwen released the man's wrist. Al thumped him on the back.

Derek couldn't express how grateful and relieved he was that Al seemed better than the last time he'd seen him. Derek pulled back to look into the man's brown eyes. "Do you feel well enough to travel to Kampala to see the race?"

Al shook his head. "Not this time."

Though disappointment spiraled through Derek, Al showed no sign of regret. The man's quiet acceptance of life's circumstance's humbled Derek. "I'm sorry, man. I know how much you were looking forward to seeing Tito race."

Al shrugged. "There will be other times. You and Tito will both win."

"Yeah, I'll give it a shot," he replied, without any real heat in his voice.

His desire to run, to win, lacked any conviction. He'd never felt so apathetic about a race before. The last twenty-four hours must have affected him more than he'd thought. In the wake of being kidnapped, a marathon seemed so unimportant.

They chatted with Tito for a few minutes before heading back to the clinic. Derek told himself he should go for a run, get ready for the race, but he just couldn't dredge up any enthusiasm.

"What's that frown for?" Gwen asked as she slipped her arm through his.

Surprise and pleasure unfurled in his chest at the gesture. "I was just thinking I should take at least one more training run before Moses and I head for Kampala."

"Ah," she said.

He studied her pensive profile. "Just *ah?* No lecture on the dangers of the bush? No demands that I not go alone?"

One side of her sweet mouth rose. "No."

"You don't care anymore? I'm wounded."

She squeezed his arm. "I care, but you're a big boy who knows the dangers out there. I trust you'll take the right precautions."

"You trust me? Be still my heart," he quipped, needing to keep things light. Her words were like sweet honey to his soul because she didn't give her trust easily.

She stopped to stare at him, her expression serious. "Yes, I trust you. In fact, I like you. You're a good guy, even if you don't believe that."

His heart began to pound in an unsteady bang. "Why wouldn't I believe that?"

"I don't know. You tell me."

He scoffed. They'd already covered this ground. "I'm going for a run. I'll be back later." He stalked away and told himself not to feel bad for the flash of hurt he saw in her eyes.

* * *

Gwen watched Derek and Tito take off down the path and disappear into the thick underbrush. Derek's powerful legss pumped with grace and his whole body moved forward in such a rhythm of beauty. A sad cloak descended on her shoulders. He was still running.

She told herself to let it go. She didn't need the headache. But the constant way he dodged anything even remotely personal about himself nagged at her.

She busied herself with the clinic but in the back of her mind the problem of Derek stayed close to the surface.

Sometime later as she showed a young mother the benefits of diaper cream, her mind had a moment of clarity, like the flash of a camera, catching a single second in clear form. Putting her mind on hold, she finished up with the woman and her child before telling Ethan she needed a break.

Once outside, she let her mind go back to the night that she and Derek had spent tied together. Something he had said struck her now as an important insight into the pain she sensed in him.

Hey, we're your typical American dysfunctional family. Workaholic father, overcompensating mother and insecure kid. Enough said.

At the time, all she'd been able to think about was how she'd have given anything for his childhood. Compared to hers, his was a dream, a fantasy that would never have come true for her.

But now she realized he'd revealed to her the source of his wounds.

Dr. Harper was a workaholic. He stayed in the clinic for long periods of time, never took vacations and rarely came home on holidays. And she'd only been at the clinic for three years. Obviously, Dr. Harper had been doing this for a long time.

Gwen kicked at the red dirt. She didn't know Mrs. Harper well, though she could see she was kind and giving. Gwen could imagine Mrs. Harper probably tried to make up for her husband's flaw by overcompensating, as Derek put it.

But Derek insecure?

He sure got touchy when she'd told him she thought he was a good guy.

He claimed he didn't "do" relationships.

She snorted under her breath. She didn't "do" relationships, either, so who was she to judge.

Except that…she'd told Derek of her past in the hopes of healing him.

And God had healed her enough to allow Derek's touch to be a comfort rather than a source of fear.

Fear had controlled her for too long. She bent her head to ask God for His forgiveness. She wanted God in control of her life. Only Him.

A shiver started in her soul and worked its way outward. For the first time she wanted to have a relationship. A relationship with Derek.

But how could she if he didn't let her in?

Derek threw his pack into the back of the jeep. He was going to buy Moses another van as soon as they got to Kampala to replace the one they'd left at the rebel camp. He doubted the rebels would take the trouble to return it.

"Have a good race," Joyce said.

She stood with Craig and Ned watching him get ready to leave. All three of them had come out of the clinic to see him off. Only Gwen was nowhere in sight. Not that he expected her to say goodbye after the way he'd treated her earlier. He'd pushed her away in self-defense.

"You guys take care. I'll see you in a few days," he said with a wave before climbing into the passenger seat. Tito sat behind Moses. The youth's knees were drawn up almost to his chest because of the limited legroom.

Moses started the engine just as the back door opened and someone slid into the seat behind Derek.

"Okay, boys let's go."

Derek jerked around and stared at Gwen. She gave him a cocky grin and adjusted her wide-brimmed cotton hat more securely on her head.

"What do you think you're doing?"

"Going to Kampala. What's it look like?"

"You're needed here."

"I'll be coming back with Moses. I need to pick up some more supplies that we're running low on."

He didn't like the idea of her not safely tucked away at the clinic. After their ordeal one would think she'd be a bit more wary of leaving. But as he'd discovered, Gwen was a strong woman with a mind of her own. A mind he admired greatly.

He forced his attention to the scenery. He'd made this trip before but now he saw it in a different light. He saw the goodness of the people, the hardships the Africans endured. And he saw the way he had taken his life and the luxuries in it for granted.

He loved the way the different trees grew. Some in clusters, dense and tightly packed with thick foliage. The occasional lone tree, majestic in its simplicity with its canopy of leaves offered precious shade.

"Look," Gwen exclaimed, placing a hand on his shoulder.

He was taken more with the warm, gentle pressure of her palm than the sight of the animal that stood stock-still in the middle of the wide grasslands. "Looks like you."

She hit his shoulder. "Excuse me?"

He chuckled. "I mean the coloring. He's red-and-white."

She made a noise in the back of her throat and sat back.

"That is a kob," explained Moses.

"Looks like an antelope," Gwen commented.

"Similar," Moses agreed.

The kob stood tall and proud as he watched them drive by. His long ringed horns had sharp points that Derek imagined could impale their vehicle clean through if it wanted to.

Derek glanced over his shoulder at Gwen. "I didn't mean to offend you."

She eyed him for a moment before giving him a smile that curled his toes. He blinked as she sat forward again and began to ask Moses questions about other wildlife they saw.

Derek loved the little bursts of delight she gave when Moses slowed the jeep down so she could see a warbler that landed on the branch of a bush beside the road. And when she pointed to a tree that sat perched on the top of a grassy hill.

"Baobab tree."

She giggled. "Looks like it was ripped from the ground and put back in upside down."

Derek chuckled. He never would have thought to describe the jumble of spiny bare branches pointing haphazardly in the air in such a vivid way.

She asked Derek about the race, about the other people he might know who were competing. The genuine interest in her eyes felt good and he found the time passing all too quickly.

Once in Kampala, they parked near the hotel where Derek would stay for the night. The race started at sunrise. A bus would pick him and the other competitors up an hour before dawn. Derek couldn't wait to take a real shower and sleep on a real mattress.

He grabbed his things from the jeep. "Thanks for driving me in."

Moses nodded and they shook hands.

Gwen stared at him for a moment, her eyes big and unreadable. "I know you'll do well."

He shrugged off her words. "Thanks. I'll try."

She stepped closer and took his face between her slender, strong hands. "No, really. I believe in you."

His breath caught somewhere between his lungs and his heart. No one had ever said that to him before. He didn't know what to say. Then she knocked the wind right out of him altogether when she went on tiptoe and pulled him closer. Very gently she pressed her lips to his.

The kiss was sweet and touching and over way too fast.

She stepped back.

He stepped forward. "What was that?"

"A good-luck kiss?"

There was such uncertainty in her beautiful eyes that he couldn't stop himself from capturing her face in his hands.

"This," he said as he bent closer, "is a kiss."

Then he kissed her deeply. She curled her fingers into his shirt and tugged him closer. He slipped one hand around her head to cup the back of her neck. He wanted to wipe away the memories of her past and create memories of their own.

Moses's and Tito's chuckle snapped Derek back to reality.

What was he thinking? Memories of their own? He didn't do commitment. Or relationships. He never wanted to have to choose between his own wants and those of someone else. He didn't want to disappoint anyone, most of all Gwen.

He broke the contact but couldn't help the sense of male satisfaction rippling through him at the dazed and flushed expression on Gwen's pretty face.

She blinked. "That was definitely a kiss."

He tugged on her braid. "I'll see you in a few days."

"Be careful," she said before turning away and climbing into the front seat of the jeep.

He stood there on the sidewalk, watching the jeep weave into the congested traffic and thought about the look in her eyes as she'd said be careful. Her words weren't a bossy command or even those of a manager to an employee, but rather words of affection.

As if she really did care.

Oh, boy.

He didn't know what to do about that. He dreaded seeing that hopeful, eager look in her eyes that said she wanted forever. He'd been down that road once and the pain he'd caused had cut him deeply. He didn't ever want to hurt Gwen like that.

Inside the hotel room, he showered and changed, but he didn't find himself enjoying the accommodations as he thought he would. The room was a standard room. No frills, just a bath, bed, table and chairs. Like any other room in America.

Only he wasn't in America. And there were villagers full of people who had no water.

Something had to be done.

I believe in you. Gwen's words. A balm to his soul.

A logical voice inside his head said to stay out of it. He'd made enough of a mess as it was trying to help. But his heart told him to step out in faith and figure out a better way.

He went to the lobby and asked the hotel concierge for directions to the Ugandan parliament. He hadn't been able to break the dam down himself, but he sure could use his clout as Executive Director of Hands of Healing to at least get an audience with someone who could help.

The parliament building was closed when he arrived. He'd have to wait until after his race to make an appointment. A few more hours wouldn't make a difference, he told himself as he walked through the evening rush of people in the heart of Kampala.

But it would.

He returned to the parliament building,

took a seat on the steps outside the huge wrought-iron gate and waited for daylight.

"You're back?"

"Good morning to you, too, Ned," Gwen replied without turning to look at the doctor. Instead she continued to scrub the already clean examination table.

When she and Moses had returned to the village the night before it had been late and she'd gone directly to bed without saying hello to anyone. But she hadn't slept much.

Her thoughts kept replaying those last few moments with Derek. The stunned expression in his green eyes when she'd told him she believed in him, almost as if that was the first time anyone had said that to him. But surely his parents had.

Oh, and then that kiss.

Not the chaste kiss she'd given him, which had seemed pretty good until he'd captured her mouth again. Her lips still tingled. The best part had been that she hadn't felt afraid.

"You should be at the finish line," Ned stated as he came to stand beside the table. He wore the green surgical scrubs he was fond of and a straw hat on his balding head. His brown eyes regarded her with worry.

Gwen gathered up the rags. "I'm needed here."

Ned's hand shot out to still her. She stared at the place where his pale, delicate surgeon's hand touched her forearm and felt…just the cool temperature of his skin.

She blinked, confused. For too long the mere touch of a male human made her skin crawl and produced the need to back away.

But now that didn't happen.

The awakening knowledge that she was truly healed sent joy cascading through her. She wanted to laugh and cry all at the same time. She wanted to tell Derek because it had started with him.

The joy subsided a bit. She contemplated Ned. "Why should I be at the finish line? Derek didn't ask any of us to be there."

Ned regarded her with a stern gaze. "You matter to him."

She laughed off his words. "Hardly."

"Listen." Ned took a deep breath and slowly let it out. "I've watched the way he has tried to get your attention from the first day he stepped into the clinic. I've seen the way he watches you when you aren't looking. Since we've been here, he's worked hard to earn your approval. I watched the way you've grown in the last few weeks. You're less rigid and more spontaneous. You smile more and even laugh. You blush when you talk with Derek. Moses told me about how protective of you Derek has been. And about the kiss."

She sucked in a breath as heat crept up her neck. Her mind struggled to process what was happening. Not only was Ned talking in long, complex sentences, but the things he was saying…she hadn't realized she'd been rigid. Or that she blushed. Or… any of it.

Had Derek really been watching her?

"You should be at that finish line when Derek crosses it. That would mean the world to him," Ned finished.

It would mean the world to her to see him accomplish his goal.

"Okay." She could be spontaneous. "Okay!"

Derek paced the outer office of the Honorable Grace Okuman. After having been sent from office to office trying to find the right division to hear his case, he'd been directed to Legal and Parliamentary Affairs.

The door opened and a woman stepped out. She had shoulder-length dark hair and was dressed in a navy business suit, with a skirt. Her mocha skin was smooth and very few wrinkles lined her intelligent eyes as she smiled, showing even white teeth. "Mr. Harper, please come in."

Derek entered and she closed the door behind him. The office was furnished in an understated collection of mahogany furniture. A large desk dominated one side of the room. Shelves filled with volumes of books lined the walls. Two wingback chairs sat facing the desk.

The woman indicated for Derek to take one of the seats as she went around behind the desk and sat in a cloth-covered task chair.

She steepled her hands on the desk. "What can the Ugandan government do for you today?"

Having explained the issue of the blocked river to everyone he'd met with this morning, he was surprised she didn't already know. "The river that runs through the province of Moswani has been barricaded by the rebels. The villages along the river have been without water for many months. I know exactly where the blockade is and have come to you to ask for your help in freeing the water."

She nodded her head in contemplation. "Yes, we had heard there were issues with the river."

Derek gritted his teeth. "*Issues* is putting

it mildly. People are suffering. Something needs to be done."

"I agree with you," she said. "You must understand that our government has many such issues to deal with and we only have so many resources. The fighting in the north takes a great deal of our manpower."

"But the fighting is now spreading. Surely, you can help the people of Moswani."

"It's not as simple as that. The Moswani people want their independence from the Ugandan government."

"I don't believe that's true. All the people we have treated over the last two weeks are not looking to break from Uganda."

"Ah, yes. You are with Hands of Healing. Our government is very grateful for the work you do."

"Thank you, but what the people need is the water from the river. At the site of the dam there is a small armed force."

She regarded him steadily for a moment. "You say you can pinpoint where these rebels are located?"

"Yes. In fact, I have a map," he said

and from the pocket of his shirt pulled out the folded race map. He spread it out on the desktop.

"This is a race map," she stated and stared at him quizzically. "Why are you not running in today's race?"

"Because this is more important," he stated simply.

She gave him a pleased smile. He showed her on the map where he and Gwen had entered the dry riverbed. "The blockade is a few miles upstream."

"Can I have this map?"

"Yes, please take it. Will you help us?"

The Honorable Grace Okuman stood. "Yes. We will deal with this. You can expect the water by the day's end."

He pumped her hand enthusiastically. "Thank you."

"The Ugandan government thanks *you*."

Derek left the parliament building with a light step. He couldn't wait to tell Gwen.

Chapter Fourteen

Gwen, Moses and Ned clapped without much enthusiasm as the last of the runners crossed the finish line. Where was Derek?

Tito had crossed the finish line ages ago in second place behind an American. She ran over to where Tito stood talking with the winner.

"Where's Derek?" she asked.

"Good question," said the American.

He introduced himself as Owen—she didn't catch the last name. Her mind was racing. Did they need to go search the trails for him?

"Mr. Derek didn't show up at the start line," Tito said.

"What?"

She turned to Ned and Moses as they approached. "Tito said he didn't start the race," she said, her voice wavering.

"Should check his hotel," Ned stated quietly as they moved away from the throng of celebrating people.

That sounded like a good idea. Unfortunately, when they arrived at the hotel, they discovered that Derek had checked out of his room a few hours earlier.

"He probably went back to the village," Moses offered as they all climbed back in the jeep.

"Maybe." Gwen couldn't understand it. Why wouldn't he have run his race? He'd trained so hard. It had seemed so important to him.

They made the long drive back to the village. When they arrived, a new minivan was parked in front of the clinic. Gwen jumped out and ran inside. She skidded to a halt at the welcome sight of Derek sitting with Craig, Joyce and Ethan. He wore a dress shirt and slacks. She hadn't even known he'd brought such nice clothing with him.

He smiled as he rose from the folding chair. "Hey, I heard you went to see the race. How'd Tito do?"

"We went to see you win. Tito came in second," she stated.

"Good for him. I had something more important to do."

He didn't look regretful or bummed to have missed the race. "Like what?"

"Let me show you." He took her by the elbow and led her outside.

She glanced back and was met with big grins from the others. She allowed him to lead her down the path he'd so often disappeared down when he went running. "Where are we going?"

"Trust me."

He halted at the dry, dusty riverbed. Brown grass stuck up in tuffs here and there. The acacia palms lining the embankment looked withered and dry. "Okay, what's going on?"

He released her elbow and grabbed her around the waist. She squealed in surprise as he spun her in a circle. "Stop! I'll get sick," she exclaimed with a laugh.

He came to a halt and set her feet on the ground but he didn't release her. "I spent the day at the Ugandan parliament building trying to get someone to help us. Finally, this wonderful lady said she'd help."

"What are you talking about?"

"The river. Since I failed at taking down the blockade myself, I went to those who could."

"Ah."

Disappointment at her lack of enthusiasm stopped him cold. "Ah? That's all you can say?"

"That's great."

Derek frowned. Why wasn't she more pleased? "The villagers will have water soon."

"I'm ecstatic. It's amazing. You're the hero."

He released her and stepped back, his heart withering. "Why the sarcasm?"

She closed her eyes for a moment as if gathering her patience before looking at him with a gentle expression. "I am really, really thankful and happy about the water. I know everyone will be. And I'm proud of you. I know what a sacrifice you made. But Derek, you are not a failure because you couldn't take the dam down yourself."

Wariness colored his vision. He had a feeling she was going to start on him again. Try to analyze him. She should have gone into psychology. "Right. We should get back and help the others start to pack up the clinic."

He only got a few paces away before her softly spoken words halted him in his tracks.

"You're still running."

Derek slowly pivoted on the edge of the riverbank. Dry grass brushed against his legs. He'd done everything he could to try to help. To try to please Gwen and still he failed. His temper flared. "What do you want from me?"

There was almost an imperceptible note of pleading in her expressive face. "I don't want anything from you, Derek, that you're not willing to give."

He frowned, sensing a trap of some sort there at the edges of his mind. Gwen would never use manipulation or deceit, but somehow her words felt confining, as if a boundary line had been drawn. "I don't know what you mean by that."

She came to him. Determined, confident, beautiful. She put her hand over his heart. "I don't know where you got the idea that you had to *earn* people's respect or their love. You have to stop looking for your self-worth in what you do or how you please others."

His defenses rose at the suggestion he was hiding from motivations that stemmed from a need to placate others. "I work hard, push myself physically to please myself." He backed away. "You are way off base."

"Am I?" She cocked her head to the side and regarded him intently. "I don't think so. I think you've spent your life trying to get your father's attention by being a winner."

He reared back, her words stinging. He hated that what she said was true. He'd done everything within his power—excelled at school and sports—to gain his father's attention. "That doesn't mean I'm trying to earn anyone's love."

She gave a look that said "Yeah, right!" "That's the thing, Derek. You can't earn people's love, sometimes it comes to you just because of who you are."

Her expressive eyes held compassion, understanding and a tenderness that chipped away at his defensive armor. He didn't want to disappoint her but he couldn't accept that he could be loved unconditionally.

"And," she continued, her voice taking on a determined edge, "you can't find your sense of self in other people. Only in God can you find your identity, and He is the only one you have to please. He gives us the freedom to choose how we respond and react to what happens to us in this world." She spread her arms wide in a gesture that encompassed the dry, dusty riverbed, the brown-and-yellow grass and the thirsty trees lining the banks of the river. "Your sense of self-worth is your responsibility."

His throat tightened, blocking his airways. He fought for breath, his mind scrambling with a crazy mixture of hope and fear. "I am not doing this," he ground out and moved to turn away. She stopped him with a hand on his arm.

"You can't run your whole life. One day you'll wake up old and alone and regret that you never let anyone in," she said softly with a touch of sadness in her eyes.

He curled his lip in defiance. "I let you in."

She rolled her eyes and let out an exasperated sigh. "You may have opened the door a little, but you promptly shut me out as soon as I tried to step through."

His heart began to pound and his lungs constricted. *Shut me out.* He shook his head as the words bounced around in his mind, turning into the echo of something he didn't want to hear.

Don't shut me out. A chorus of female

voices, Jenny's and more than a dozen other women over the years, all saying the same thing.

Now Gwen was saying the same thing.

His breathing sounded labored in his ears. His heart hammered painfully in his chest as if he'd just run a ten-kilometer uphill in high altitude. He held her gaze. He didn't see forever—a lifetime of commitment—in her eyes but he did see her heart. Her generous, compassionate heart. The heart of a doctor wanting to heal.

"You can't fix me, Gwen," he said harshly to hide the sadness and the regret burrowing into his soul. No matter how skilled she was or even if she had some cure-all pill, she couldn't make a difference.

"Why not? You fixed me," she quietly replied.

He swallowed. "What?"

She stepped closer. "I've lived so long in fear. Fear of being touched, fear of intimacy. Afraid that I'd never be a normal woman with normal desires." Her gaze shifted to her dirt-covered feet.

His heart contracted in his chest at the thought of what she'd endured and had lived with for so long.

Her chin lifted, courage and resolve shining bright in her gaze. "God brought you into my life to heal me."

He wanted to believe she was right, that God had brought them together for a reason. For her healing. Yeah, maybe. But that didn't mean he needed to be healed and that she was the one to do it. No one could.

"I thought when this journey started that my promise to your father was the only thing between us. I was wrong. There's a lot between us," she added as she reached out once again to touch his arm.

He focused on one word. Every muscle in his body contracted. What game was she playing? Had they been scheming against him? "Promise?"

"He loves you a great deal, Derek."

He didn't want to hear about his father's love. She couldn't understand how hard it was to believe when nothing he'd done had been enough.

"Your father made me promise I'd help you see the importance of our work here."

Her words hurt worse than the blow he'd sustained to the side of his head. Doubt flooded him. "So all your attention to me, all your pushing at me, was for my father? Now who's the pleaser?"

"It started out that way." She gazed up at him, the tender expression in her eyes cutting through him. "But it turned out to be so much more."

Oh, man. He couldn't let her or himself go down that dead-end road. "I'm sorry, Gwen. There can't be more," he stated in a monotone and felt as if his heart was being ripped from his chest.

"Why? Because you can't trust my motives?"

He swiped a hand through his hair. Gwen's heart was pure, just filled with misguided loyalty. "No, that's not it."

She took his hand, the warmth of her skin chased his pain all the way to his heart.

"Don't be afraid of love," she said, her voice fragile and shaky.

"It's not love that scares me," he rasped out. "It's… it's knowing that I'll fail. And I don't want to see the hurt and disappointment that failure will cause."

Her eyes narrowed. "The only way you'll fail is if you don't love. You'll fail yourself. You'll fail God, because He made you to love." She once again placed her hand over his heart, her palm burning clear through.

"I've seen the person you try to hide," she continued. "You are so capable of great love. I've watched you with Cam, saw the bond you formed with him. I've seen the camaraderie you have with Tito and the others. The only way you could ever disappoint anyone is by denying your ability to love, by holding yourself apart."

He staggered beneath the weight of need her words heaped on his heart. He didn't want to hear, to believe it could be so easy and simple when all his life letting himself care only brought pain and heartache. He wanted to get away from her and her words. He wanted to…run away.

He hung his head in shame and regret. He *had* been running from love. Over and over again, whenever love came too close, he'd bolt because he couldn't bear the thought of not measuring up. He saw that now.

Trouble was he didn't know what to do about it.

Gwen watched the play of emotions etch themselves in Derek's handsome features. Disbelief, horror, shame, acceptance and self-doubt. Her heart throbbed with empathy. Every word she'd said had been true and he was a strong enough man to handle it.

He could handle anything. That was how much faith and trust she had in him.

Beneath her palm his heart pounded erratically. Her own heart was flopping around in her chest trying to tell her something, but she kept her focus on Derek, on her need to heal him.

"Let the past go, Derek."

He raised his moist gaze to her. Answering tears gathered in her eyes forming a lump in the back of her throat. She swallowed and forced herself to continue. "Forgive your father for not being the father you wanted and needed. Forgive yourself for letting fear control you. I've forgiven myself for the fear, and let me tell you, it's liberating."

He frowned, his gaze razor sharp. "You can't compare what happened to you with my measly hang-ups."

"If it's keeping you from loving, then it's exactly the same. You have to learn to give yourself a break."

His face became a study of contemplation. She could see his mind weighing her words, turning them over for analysis. He was smart and she had no doubt he'd see the value of the truth she spoke.

"I'll give it a shot," he said, his voice betraying a hesitation to commit to the healing process.

She had to make him see that it would take more than just a halfhearted attempt. He had to go the distance. "But you have to start letting people in, otherwise the fear still wins. And that is one race you can't afford to lose."

He reached out and touched her braid, sending her senses reeling. The sight of his big, tanned hand holding her hair was a powerful draw and she fought the urge to bury herself in his embrace. Doing so would push him away.

"Who do you suggest I let in first, Gwennie?"

Her heart stalled and then galloped toward some distant finish line. She wanted to rein it in, to control the course she took, but she realized with a clarity that was beyond herself that she wanted Derek to let her in completely, desperately. And the reason flagged her down.

She loved him. With all her heart.

A shiver of anxiety washed over her. Loving and being loved were such unpredictable forces. What if he didn't love her back? Could she take that?

Only one way to find out. She had to risk relinquishing control of her destiny to him. Let him decide if he'd let her in.

Or not.

She took a deep, steadying breath. "I…I hope you'll let me in," she managed to whisper.

His fingers tugged at the band holding her hair together. He might as well have been undoing the bands around her heart.

"Why?" His voice seemed to touch her.

He distracted her completely by taking the band off and running his fingers through her hair, undoing the tight braid.

"Gwennie?"

"Hmm?" She glanced up, falling into his intense gaze.

His green eyes were no longer moist, but shone with a determined, probing light. "Why do you want me to let you in?"

Words formed, but wouldn't materialize. Old habits of holding back were hard to break. But her life, her heart hung in the balance. She would not fail to fight for what she wanted. What she needed.

"I love you," she stated simply and prayed he felt the same.

What if he doesn't? Will the risk be worth it?

* * *

Derek stilled, his fingers caught in the mass of red wavy hair now cascading over Gwen's shoulder. He looked into her eyes and finally saw the light of forever in their amber depths.

"What if I disappoint you?" He whispered the question, hating that he couldn't just give himself over to her love.

"If I have expectations that you don't live up to, that's my problem. I get to decide whether I allow myself to be disappointed."

He took a shuddering breath. "I'm just no good at relationships."

She grabbed his face, her palms making imprints on his jaw. "Only because you've been too worried about failing, about disappointing. Let that go. Concentrate, instead, on loving and being loved."

He waited, expecting to feel panicked, trapped. Amazingly, a joyous burst of adrenaline coursed through him, pushing him on to race headlong into that light and embrace his future.

He pulled her to him, holding her as if she'd disappear.

He stroked her glorious hair and let the healing power of her love work its wonders on his soul. She was right that he couldn't look to others for his self-worth. God gave him the choice to feel worthy or not. Her wisdom never ceased to astound him. And he loved that about her.

He loved her.

Throwing back his head with a freeing laugh, he picked her up and swung her around again. Her laughter filled his soul to bursting. He set her on her feet and captured her face in his hands.

"Gwennie. I love you, too. And I want forever with you."

The smile of joy on her freckled face beamed as bright as the sun and warmed him to his very depths. A loud rushing filled his ears as he bent to claim her with his kiss.

Suddenly fresh river water swirled around their feet, getting deeper with each passing second. The water finally arrived. Tufts of grass sticking up through the dry dirt bent as if in appreciation of the flowing water. The village would be saved. But more than that, the water was washing away the past and bringing a purity to their future.

A future he'd never imagined.

Epilogue

Derek, Gwen discovered, had a lot of affection and love to give, and she relished the basking glow of his care. She thought at first she'd be embarrassed by Derek's demonstrative, though infinitely respectful, attention, but the whole team had approved and accepted the fact that they were an item. As if she and Derek were the last to figure it out.

The trip back to the States was a fun and relaxing journey, even though she already missed her friends in Africa.

She enjoyed the weight of Derek's arm around her shoulders as they came through their planes Jetway and out to their gate at Sea-Tac Airport. Only two weeks since they'd left for Africa and her life had changed so much. But so much for the better.

She'd never expected to find love, to be able to let down the barriers that kept her world controlled and safe. She never dreamed she'd give her heart to her boss's son.

"Derek! Gwen!"

Gwen glanced around and saw Dr. Harper hobbling over to them on crutches. The pant leg of his charcoal-colored dress slacks was tucked inside his cast. The white oxford button-down and tie made him look distinguished. Mrs. Harper hurried alongside her husband, her navy pumps clicking on the linoleum floor. She wore a flowered skirt and a jersey top.

Dr. Harper's eyes widened with interest as he took in his son's arm around his protégé's shoulders. Then his lined face broke out into a huge grin. "I knew it!"

Gwen waited for Derek to tense up, but he didn't, and pride in him made her squeeze him with the arm she had around his waist. Derek squeezed her back before breaking away to engulf his father in a bear hug.

Surprise flashed in Dr. Harper's eyes before they misted with unmistakable joy. He dropped the crutches to embrace his son. Gwen felt her own eyes tear up. She achieved her goal and fulfilled her promise beyond her wildest imaginings.

Father and son looked happy together.

When the two men broke apart, Derek gave his mother a hug and kiss. He returned his attention to his father. "You knew what?"

Incredibly, Dr. Harper flushed, guilty. "I knew you two would be great together if given a chance."

"Really?" Derek cocked a brow. "Do you hear that, Gwennie? Dad was playing matchmaker."

Dr. Harper and his wife exchanged conspiratorial glances.

Gwen laughed and went to hug her boss as Derek bent to pick up the crutches lying on the floor. "Well, it worked."

Dr. Harper held her fast and murmured in her ear. "Thank you. He deserved a woman like you."

She leaned back to look into his dear, craggy face. "Thank God, not me."

He nodded in understanding and took the crutches from Derek. "So, tell me everything that happened."

Gwen and Derek exchanged a long stare. So much had happened. It would take a long time to tell their story. A lifetime that she looked forward to spending with Derek.

She slipped into Derek's embrace and found the best shelter.

In his heart.

* * * * *

Dear Reader,

Thank you for going on this life-changing journey with Gwen and Derek as they discover love while touching lives in Africa. Though Moswani and Hands of Healing are both fictional, the plight of the African nations and the organizations that do bring relief aid are not. What better way of showing God's love than reaching out to bring comfort and help to those in need? If you would like information on ways you can help, let me introduce you to some organizations that I am personally involved with: Good Samaritan Ministries, www.gsmusa.org and Northwest Medical Teams, www.nwmedicalteams.org.

May God bless you,

QUESTIONS FOR DISCUSSION

1. What made you want to read this book? Did it live up to your expectations?

2. Did you think Gwen and Derek were realistic characters? Talk about the secondary characters. Were they important to the story?

3. The setting was central to the story. Have you ever been to a foreign country and had a life-changing experience? How did the setting change Gwen and Derek?

4. One of the faith elements in the story was about one's sense of self-worth. How do you define yourself and where do you look for your self-worth? Do you believe that your sense of self stems from God?

5. Derek's insecurities stemmed from his relationship with his father. How does the parent/child relationship affect our adult lives? How has it affected you?

6. The trauma of Gwen's past left her scarred and controlled by fear. Have you let fear control your actions/decisions?

7. Derek and Gwen both make sacrifices and changes for love. What were those sacrifices/changes? What promoted them? What resulted from them? Have you made a sacrifice/change in your own life? When, why and what was the outcome?

8. What was the symbolism of Derek's running? What was he running from? What have you emotionally run from?

9. Did the author's use of language/writing style make this an enjoyable read? Would you read more from this author?

10. What will be your most vivid memories of this book? What lessons about life, love and faith did you learn from this story?